THE BREAD OF LIFE

The Bread of Life

Orthodox Short Stories

by

Barbara and Priscilla Johnson

Illustrated by Priscilla Johnson

ST. NECTARIOS PRESS
SEATTLE, WASHINGTON
1999

THE BREAD OF LIFE
ORTHODOX SHORT STORIES
by Barbara and Priscilla Johnson
Illustrated by Priscilla Johnson

ISBN 0-913026-48-4

Library of Congress Catalog Card Number 99-073878

Published by
ST. NECTARIOS PRESS
10300 ASHWORTH AVENUE NORTH
SEATTLE, WASHINGTON 98133-9410

Typesetting & Layout by
Apple Tree Press
Yakima, WA

Preface

With great pleasure we present what we believe to be the first book-length work of modern Orthodox fiction published in English. Why Orthodox fiction? All societies have produced literary works influenced by their culture and religious beliefs. Russia and Greece produced writers who incorporated Orthodox religious views of life in their writings. Dostoyevsky, Papadiamantis, and Bastias are among writers of the 19th and 20th century whose fictional writings have reflected an Orthodox Christian perspective. We are sure there are many others to be found in all Orthodox languages and countries.

Although not all of the stories in this volume are set in this day and age, all impart values and attitudes which are a timeless expression of Orthodox Christian life. All of them encourage us to live our faith, to become conscious participants in the common struggle for salvation. We believe that these values can be found in fiction that is entertaining and easy to read. We look forward to seeing many more such works as Orthodoxy plants its roots in the English-speaking world.

ST. NECTARIOS PRESS

Table of Contents

The Bread of Life

I will call to Me the nations,
and they shall glorify Me, with the Father and the Spirit,
and I will grant them life everlasting.

Hymn of the Royal Hours on Holy Friday

Sun, warm sun. Lowering herself slowly down to the step, wincing as her movements woke a pain in her chest, Tamar clutched her metal cup in both gnarled hands and savored the warmth. Another winter behind her; another summer ahead.

As if they sensed it, or as if they had caught what Americans called "spring fever"—which Tamar, when she had just come from Soviet Georgia, had thought was a disease—a gang of children darted shouting across the street, and Tamar tightened her fingers on her cup, bracing herself in case they tried to snatch it from her. They did that, these brawling children. … Dodging each other's fists, they raced towards her along the sidewalk.

"Ol' bag lady! Hey, got a quarter?"

Glowering at them, Tamar hunched her shoulders, drawing her shawl closer despite the warmth. If they provoked her far enough, she would scream at them in Georgian, but a dog barking at them distracted them, and they chased off after it.

Let them go; she was glad that they went without rousing her anger, because screaming hurt her chest.

When she first came to America, when she was young and scraping by on factory wages, this had been Greektown, and the odd Greek restaurant among the crumbling storefronts tried to persuade passers-by that it still was, but the boarded-up windows of buildings and the graffiti on sidewalks and parked cars and lamp-posts told the true story.

1

2

Oh, the odd Greek still lived here, like the man who owned the bakery on whose step Tamar was sitting, while from an open window above the bakery drifted down the voices of two girls. His daughters, maybe; only one of them ever dropped her spare change in Tamar's cup. The other was too fancy to pay heed to an old Georgian woman in a threadbare shawl.

But weren't most young people like that now? Like the children who tormented Tamar, who were too wrapped up in themselves to see past her appearance, or to care.

Well, an Orthodox Christian was supposed to bear revilement, she would tell herself. Despite the hateful atheist Soviets, much of Georgia had remained Orthodox, and Tamar, when she escaped to America, had struggled to keep that.... For what? To sit on a bakery step in the poor section of a city and rattle a cup at people who walked by?

Perhaps God didn't listen to the old. Perhaps He didn't care… and she should learn to think only about herself, like the young of today. Learn to ignore Him, as it seemed He ignored her. Unless the Soviets were right after all, and He didn't exist.

As she dwelt on her thoughts, the bakery door creaked open behind her, spilling the smell of fresh bread into the street, and the baker stepped out into the sun, revealing his presence to Tamar with a hiss of breath through his nose as he approached her. "Here, you take this dollar and go buy yourself a cup of coffee, and don't come back to my step. Customers don't like to come in past you, you know that."

She knew because he told her whenever he caught her sitting there, and Tamar slanted a glance at him as she gathered her painful self off the step. Dark of hair and mustache, swarthy of skin. Georgian, which he might have passed for, or Greek, did it matter? What did anything matter? What did God matter, or Christianity, or rude youth, or the sun shining down on a city in America? Or another winter behind Tamar, or two girls chattering in an upper room? What did any of it matter?

Hobbling down the street with the Greek baker's dollar scrunched in her fist, Tamar felt the void inside of herself, and tried to concentrate on her empty stomach instead of on the aching emptiness beating behind her ribs, and knew that not even a loaf of the baker's fresh bread could fill her.

"Here, I'll wash those dishes. If you want to help, sit down and dry." As she spoke, Evgenia Vasiliou conducted her sister-in-law to the kitchen table, and Nikolia sank down with a sigh, clasping her hands around her swollen stomach.

"Just pass me the dishtowel and I won't complain."

Evgenia tossed it, watching as Nikolia reached out to catch it. "You never do complain, not even with that baby weighing you down. How much longer do you have until it's born, a month or so? I told you Papa can probably bake prosphora as well as you can, so you don't have to insist on doing it." But Nikolia would; she always did, now. Evgenia's mother had taken Nikolia under her wing and taught her how, when her mother was still there to teach…. Why did that rankle, when Evgenia had refused to learn? Who had volunteered their family to bake all the prosphora for their church anyway?

"He likes me to do it, and besides, I want to."

"Oh, I know." Turning to the sink, Evgenia removed her rings and pushed up her sleeves. "About what we were talking about: do you think I'll ever find the right person?"

"You'll find someone."

"The right one?"

Nikolia shrugged. "I suppose so. I don't really believe there's only one right spouse for each person in the world, do you? Whoever you marry, it's always a struggle."

"You know better than I do, of course." The right one–this week, at least–was a dark boy whose name Evgenia didn't even know, and who had never looked at her. Someone's grandson or nephew, visiting from Greece. Well, he would go back to Greece without looking at her, and Evgenia turned the hot water on and attacked the prosphora pans that Nikolia insisted on washing before she baked.

"Be patient, Evgenia. In God's time, everything arranges itself. How old are you anyway? Twenty-two? I was a year older than you are when I got engaged."

Which really had no bearing on the problem, Evgenia thought. Besides, Nikolia had known Peter for two years before they decided to marry, and Evgenia didn't know anyone, not anyone, that she would even consider, no matter how desperate she got. "Why do you bother washing these pans before you use them?"

"Oh… You know I found a roach once in that corner where we keep them. If you're done with that pan, let me dry it."

Trailing suds, Evgenia passed Nikolia a clean pan. "How many more times do you have to bake prosphora before Pascha?"

"Just once, after this. If I bake four now and freeze them, I'll have to bake again on Holy Saturday." Nikolia grimaced. "That's besides dying eggs and baking Paschal bread, unless you want to do that."

"Me?"

"When you get married, you'll have to cook, you know."

"I do cook, I just don't bake." Instead of *when* Evgenia got married, Nikolia should say *if*. If Evgenia ever got married. If Nikolia wouldn't fuss at her about it when she'd just finished telling her to be patient. Emphasizing that wish with a flourish of her sponge, Evgenia sent a soapy wave pouring out of the sink onto her skirt and shoes. "Oh! Oh, no, no."

"What is it?" Heaving her bulk out of her chair, Nikolia hurried to her sister-in-law. "What's wrong? It's only water. It will dry."

"No, it won't. These are hundred dollar suede shoes. Look at them, look at them! I haven't even worn them yet. I was just wearing them today for the first time. If you didn't have to wash these stupid pans, this wouldn't have happened."

"Here, try this." Reaching behind her for the dishtowel, Nikolia poised to bend down and mop the shoes, but Evgenia stepped away from her.

"You don't understand. You don't care what you wear. I think if I threw a designer skirt in your lap, you'd probably wear that old thing that you have on instead."

Her eyes down, the picture of humility, Nikolia twined the dishtowel around her hands. "That isn't true."

"Yes, it is!" Spinning on her heel, Evgenia fled from the kitchen, fled past the stairs that led down to her father's bakery, darted along a short hall to the bedrooms.

Once in her own room, she tore off her shoes and flung them out the window into the alley behind the house, grinning a tight grin as one tumbled into a trash can and the other fell into a puddle of slime. Turning away from the window, she stared at her reflection in the mirror: her dark hair brushed and curled with such care this morning, her make-up and earrings chosen to match her outfit. Ugly, ugly, ugly, she was ugly! Why did God bother to create someone so ugly?

With trembling care, she pulled her earrings out and tossed them under her dresser, and put her hands in her hair and ruffled it until the curls disappeared in tangles, and threw herself down on her bed and wept for her ruined shoes, and for her hopeless life, and for Nikolia who would be finishing the dishes and starting her baking.

Customers were in and out. In between their appearances, Michael Vasiliou busied himself wiping down the counters, and rearranging the buns and cakes and pastries in their trays, and hoping that the old beggar woman would choose some other doorstep to sit on for the rest of the day.

Uncharitable, maybe, but business was business, and she drove it away. Who wanted to walk past a ragged old woman to get into a bakery? Anyway, he had given her a dollar.

What remained for him to bake now? A wedding cake, but it would be fresher if he baked it tomorrow. Well, the muffins were low, so he should bake more of them.

Hours earlier, the morning crowd of Greek men on their way to work had come and gone: John the carpenter and John the construction worker arguing over techniques; Vasili the restaurateur ducking in for Greek coffee and pastries before he opened his restaurant for brunch; Demetrios, son of the priest, stopping in on his way to his used car dealership; Demetrios the builder informing them all that his nephew from Greece was talking about staying in America and going in with Demetrios. "He says Greece isn't so good anymore, not a country he wants to raise his children in. Too much bad TV. And he says the girls just care about outshining each other."

At that, Vasili laughed deep in his throat. "What does he think our daughters care about? He's not going to find a girl who doesn't care about looking pretty, unless he wants to marry a nun."

Too bad for Demetrios' nephew that Nikolia was taken, Michael thought. Michael's son Peter had done well in attracting her, for she was sweet and thoughtful and not obsessed with her appearance.

Evgenia, on the other hand...

If only Eleni were still here to handle her daughter. If only her death hadn't deprived Michael of wife and close friend both at once, and of his last hope of understanding Evgenia. If only he didn't still turn around sometimes thinking he heard Eleni's voice behind him, or her step on the stairs.

Thank God for Nikolia. At least Michael still had someone to bake the prosphora for the church, which he had offered to do twenty years ago as a favor to the priest, whose overworked wife had little time for such things. Baker though he was, Michael had managed to persuade Eleni to bake the prosphora instead, not telling her why, because telling her would have made her protest. The truth was, she prayed; prayed more and better than he did, and someone of prayer should bake prosphora, he had always felt. It seemed that God agreed with him, because when He took Eleni, He had provided Nikolia.

Nikolia had said something about baking today, hadn't she? If she was going to, she'd have to bake again right before Pascha, and how would she fit in the Paschal bread, which Eleni had insisted the woman of the house should bake and which Nikolia insisted on baking for Michael because Eleni had? Well, she would manage, and even if she couldn't, life was in God's hands, and Michael could bake Paschal bread if he had to, if Nikolia was needed for prosphora.

A good daughter-in-law, Nikolia, and busy carrying a grandchild, who should be born in a month or so, right around Pascha, if Michael remembered right.

Picking up a dry cloth, he wiped the counter for the thousandth time, ducking his head not to see the icon hanging on the wall in his line of sight. When he thought thoughts like, *I'm glad of Nikolia because her presence means I can just go along as I always have, praying if I remember to*, it seemed that the Mother of God looked out of her icon into his cold, unworthy soul, and wasn't pleased with what she saw there. He was a businessman, he reminded her, and six days a week he had to get up before the sun to bake. Didn't he usually make it to church before the Liturgy ended on Sundays? Wasn't that enough? It showed his dedication, didn't it?

With a sigh from his heart, he flung the cloth down. He knew he hadn't convinced the Mother of God, but by now he was too set in his ways to change himself, that was all.

"Evgenia! Evgenia?"

"What?" By now she must have read enough prayers to prepare herself for Communion, Evgenia decided as she tossed her prayerbook on her bed and turned to check her appearance in the mirror, before opening the door to confront her father. "Is it time to go already?" When did the Liturgy start? At the same time as always, or was it different on Holy Thursday?

"I just had a call from Peter."

"So?" Her father looked... stunned? Serious, yes; maybe concerned. Stunned?

When he spoke, his voice sounded sharp with emotion. "He was calling from the hospital–"

"*What!*"

"–to say that Nikolia's in labor."

"Oh, you scared me." If that was all, what did her father have to look worried about? "She'll be all right, won't she?"

"It's going fine. However."

Now the blow was coming, whatever it was, and Evgenia braced herself for it.

"She won't be able to bake prosphora or Paschal bread for the feast. So...I'll manage the prosphora, and she said to tell you to buy three dozen eggs; the red dye is in our kitchen, in the top right drawer nearest the stove, and the Paschal bread recipe is there, too. We can spend Holy Saturday baking."

Nikolia was trying to persuade Evgenia into attempting something that wouldn't succeed, she knew it wouldn't. She never baked. Eggs were one thing, but bread! "I'm not baking bread."

Her father frowned at her, but as if his thoughts weren't totally on her. "If you don't, we won't have any, because I won't have time, not while I'm baking prosphora. And the church needs those. You're an adult, so I'm going to trust you to act like one, and to do what needs to be done."

Not if it meant baking bread. Not, not, not. As much as Evgenia tried, her father refused to argue further with her, although he told her that her mother would be pleased if she baked the Paschal bread. How he knew that, Evgenia wasn't going to ask; and she stood through the Holy Thursday Liturgy in determination. She wouldn't bake any bread, Paschal or otherwise. She wouldn't.

On Holy Friday, she woke up even more determined. No bread. Let them go without, if her father couldn't fit it in. He was busy moping around, slipping out after dinner for the vigil last night, and who could tell how long he would want to stay at church today? The services lasted all day.

Well, since they were going to church, Evgenia would try to pay attention, and try to feel present at the Saviour's betrayal, when He was obedient unto death, but she wasn't going to bake the Paschal bread.

On Holy Saturday, her stubbornness carried her to the store for the eggs, and into the bakery kitchen to dye them, because her father would be working upstairs. For some reason, her mother and Nikolia always used the upstairs kitchen, the one in the house, when they baked prosphora, maybe because her father might need the down-stairs kitchen, the one attached to the bakery, to bake things to sell. Today, for some even less sensible reason, her father had decided to bake his prosphora upstairs, and had sent her down here, where she hardly knew where anything was, and where she had to keep the door shut, however hot it might get, to avoid disturbing the tempo-rary workers hired to work behind the bakery's counter for Holy Fri-day and today.

Eggs being less difficult, she managed to dye them, and only cracked one or two. Although the red dye she used streaked a little, it didn't come off on her hands too much, and she packed the eggs up and put them away in the refrigerator, and took out the bread recipe to look at.

If Nikolia thought Evgenia could do this, she didn't know Evgenia. Even if she tried it, she knew it wouldn't turn out. If her father wanted to count on her to bake this bread because there wasn't anyone else who could, he'd have to resign himself to wasting the ingredients. It wouldn't turn out.

But he was counting on her, and he was upstairs baking prosphora, which she didn't remember his ever doing before. While he was doing that, was she going to sulk?

Yes. Maybe…

Maybe not. With care, following the recipe, she measured out flour and spices, and for her father's sake attempted to make a proper dough, but she must have done something wrong, because it stuck to her hands, and to her hair when she pushed her hair out of her face, and to her sleeve when she brushed against it by accident.

This bread, if she tried to bake it, wouldn't turn out. It wasn't working, as she'd known it wouldn't. Why had she bothered with this? Why had she thought it might turn out? Who did she think she was? She never baked bread. As a baker, her father knew what he was doing, and his prosphora would turn out, while her own stupid bread…

Gathering up her dough in both hands, she flung it with all her strength into the sink, and glared at the lump of it melting there. "I can't do this, and I don't know why I thought I could." As much as she wanted to run upstairs to her room, she couldn't even do that, because her father would see her when she passed the upstairs kitchen.

If only Nikolia were here. Why couldn't the stupid baby have waited? If only someone would help Evgenia!

As she turned her eyes away from the sink, they fell on an icon of the Saviour watching her from a shelf across the room. At the sight of Him, she remembered yesterday, Holy Friday, and how He had gone obediently to death on a cross. Where was her obedience?

"I tried," she explained to Him. "I did try, You saw me try. I just can't do it. Even when I want to obey my father, I can't."

So much for obedience. Why did the Lord give Evgenia something that was too hard for her to do? Why couldn't Nikolia be here?

If she were here, what would she do? Pray, probably, asking for God's help. When something went wrong, Nikolia always prayed, but if Evgenia tried to pray, would God listen to her?

He might. Anyway, she'd just been talking to Him. Wasn't He listening then? If she thought what He had given her to do was too hard for her, shouldn't He give her the strength to do it?

So she should ask Him to help her. She should. . . and she dared a glance at His icon. Of course He would want her to do what her father expected of her. Since she couldn't, though, not by herself, maybe He would make it possible for her; even for her, who wasn't humble or good like Nikolia.

Looking away from the icon, Evgenia buried her face in her dough-covered hands. "O Lord, help me!"

A person of prayer. In order to make prosphora, it was good to be a person of prayer, as Eleni had been, or as Nikolia was. Nikolia who was in the hospital, recovering from having her baby after a day and a half of labor, and who would miss the Pascha service, and whose presence Michael missed now, as selfish as that was.

Let rise, divide, let rise, bake… Although to Michael's practiced eye the recipe for prosphora seemed clear enough, he still hadn't summoned the courage to do anything more than get out the pans.

"I'm not a man of prayer." For the past two days, from the Liturgy on Holy Thursday and the Twelve Gospels that night, through all the services of Holy and Great Friday, he had done his best to pray, asking for help in his unworthiness, but two days didn't make a man into a man of prayer, when he wasn't.

If he didn't bake these prosphora, the church wouldn't have any for the midnight Pascha service tonight, and if he didn't start soon, the prosphora wouldn't be ready in time.

So he had to start, but he sank into a chair at the kitchen table. "O Lord, help me."

Was it perhaps presumptuous of him to ask the Lord for help and expect to receive it? How was he, Michael, any different from the evil people who had crucified the Lord? Instead of heart-felt prayer, he had given the Lord lip-service. Instead of loving Him, Michael had loved the world.

"O Lord, I'm not worthy of Your help…. I'm not worthy of baking these prosphora that will be used for Your divine Eucharist."

Twenty years ago, Michael had offered his family to the Lord's service in the baking of prosphora for His church, but in all those years, Michael himself had never baked once . . . until now, when the Lord had arranged matters so that he had to. As Michael, not Eleni or Nikolia, had been the one to make that promise, so now the Lord was calling him to fulfill it, and Michael knew he wasn't prayerful enough to be worthy of the task. "O Lord, help me!"

This day, Holy Saturday, on which Christ descended into Hades, was the day on which Michael was being called to ascend from the Hades of worldly cares, or so it seemed. This was the day that the Lord called him to become a man of prayer, at least to take the first step towards prayer.

"O Lord, with Your help, maybe I can learn to pray. I'm a Greek, one of the nations that You called to Your service, and I want to serve You, but I'm weak. Raise me up, the sinner, and fill me with godly strength. Please, of Your mercy."

As he said those words, Michael felt his unease flowing out of him, and a remembrance of Eleni came to him. Before she began her prosphora, she had always lit a candle in front of the icons in the kitchen and read an Akathist to the Mother of God, and as she baked, she left the candle burning to remind herself of prayer. If Michael did the same, with the Lord's help, how far wrong could he go?

Let rise, divide, let rise, bake . . . As well as he could, Michael prayed while he worked, and by the time the prosphora came from the oven, he felt scoured clean, with his past behind him and a future closer to God, he hoped, ahead of him; and who knew, maybe Nikolia would be too busy with her new baby to bake prosphora, and Michael would have to do it from now on.

Sighing, he wrapped the warm prosphora in cloths and set them out to cool, and remembering Evgenia, summoned the strength to go down to the bakery kitchen and see how her bread had turned out. If she'd baked at all, that was, and Michael smiled at himself, because he hadn't wanted to bake any more than she had. Maybe she would have liked to switch places? With Paschal bread, he was more sure of his skill, but he had trouble imagining Evgenia agreeing to bake prosphora.

"Evgenia?" Stepping into the bakery kitchen, Michael saw first the loaves of Greek Paschal bread cooling on his industrial racks, each loaf with a red egg baked into it. After them, he saw Evgenia hunched in a chair, her face hidden in her apron, her pretty clothes spotted with flour and dough, and more dough in the darkness of her hair.

Crying? Was she? "Evgenia, what is it? The bread looks perfect. I knew you could do it."

With a shuddering sigh, she emerged from her apron, red-nosed, her cheeks streaked with flour and tears. "I didn't. It was a mess, not turning out at all, and then I prayed, and it got better. I didn't want to do this at all, and I don't know how it's going to taste, but I did it. How are your prosphora?"

"With God's help, I think they're all right." Such bakers they were, the two of them, and he was one by profession, but that hadn't stopped him from needing God's help, as she said she had needed it. Perhaps she was more like him than he had realized, and so maybe he could learn to understand her, even though he didn't have Eleni here to help him. Anyway, God would always help, if He was asked with fervent prayer. "Now, don't cry. God helped both of us, and we should be glad about that."

"I *am* glad, and I'm not crying. I mean, I don't want to. It's just so silly." Somewhere Evgenia found a smile. "I was so busy not wanting to bake this bread, and thinking I couldn't, when all I had to do was ask God for His mercy. I don't know why I didn't think of it before."

Because the world intruded, clouding men's thinking and turning them away from God, Michael thought, and because no one wanted to admit he was helpless before God, even if everyone was.

Reaching out for Evgenia, Michael drew her out of her chair and into his arms. "Well, you asked God, and so did I, and that's what counts. And if you want to know what I think, I think you'd better go wash the flour off your face."

"Oh, Papa!"

But Evgenia was still smiling, leaning into Michael's embrace, and he bent his head and kissed her dough-tangled hair. "And I'll go up and see how my prosphora are doing. And then we can think about eating something and resting before the midnight service."

"All right, as long as I don't have to bake anything more." Freeing herself from Michael, Evgenia reached up and removed a bit of dough from his mustache. "Now you have flour on your face too, from hugging me."

As she disappeared up the stairs, Michael rubbed at his mustache, thinking thoughts about daughters and bread and prayers, and glanced at Evgenia's bread cooling on his racks, and then at the icon of the

Saviour on its shelf. "O Lord, Your mercy has touched both of us, Evgenia and me. Thank You."

"It is the day of Resurrection..." Smiling, Evgenia reached for the closest dress, blue and white like the Greek flag, radiant like today. "...let us be radiant all ye peoples, Pascha, the Lord's Pascha!"

A run of the brush through her dark hair, and no make-up, because who needed it? Instead of her usual prayers, usually rushed, she would read the Paschal Hours, and she could take as long as she wanted about it, because all she had to do today was pack up a loaf of Paschal bread for Demetrios the builder's wife, and wait for whomever Demetrios would send to pick her up for the Paschal lamb-feast.

"I'll see that he sends someone," her father had told her over a breakfast of red eggs and cheese and bread, before he left to help Demetrios and the other men of the parish get the lamb started roasting. "Probably one of his nephews, he has such a lot of them. You're lucky he's having the lamb-feast at his house this year, because if Vasili were doing it like last year, you'd have to walk. All his nephews are in Greece, and his son's only seven."

"Papa," she had protested, and her father had smiled at her.

After her prayers, she went down to the bakery to pack up the Paschal bread. Tomorrow her father would be selling what loaves remained to other Greeks or to intrigued Americans, but today they all reposed in the refrigerator, and she took one out and carried it into the bakery, hoping to find clean wax-coated paper there to wrap it in.

Outside of the bakery, on the step, Evgenia caught sight of the old beggar woman who so often sat there, although Evgenia's father had asked her not to; asked her more times than Evgenia could count. *Stupid old woman*, she thought, and then, glancing at her father's icon of the Mother of God, whose eyes seemed to look into Evgenia's heart: *No, I didn't mean that. I shouldn't have said it. Now I suppose I ought to give the old woman something, to make up for it.* Of course, the woman didn't know Evgenia's thoughts, but even so. Nikolia always gave her her spare change, saying, "If I were poor and lived on the streets, I would be thankful for anyone who took pity on me."

Whether Evgenia had any money or not remained to be seen.

Patting her pockets, she discovered them empty. Well, so she had nothing to give but the bread in her hands, which she accounted hers because she had made it, but no one gave Paschal bread to beggars. No one that she had ever heard of did.

"O holy Mother of God, what should I do? All I have is this bread, but I wanted to give the old woman something because I thought bad thoughts about her."

Why not give her the bread? the answer seemed to come back to Evgenia. It would save the old woman the trouble of trying to buy food for herself with any spare change Evgenia might have come up with to give her.

All right. Her mind made up, Evgenia picked up the bread and marched to the bakery door, unlocked and opened it, and advanced on the old woman sitting on the step, who stumbled to her feet when she saw Evgenia coming, but Evgenia held out a hand to her. "Wait, don't go yet. I – um – I wanted to give you this." Into the woman's gnarled old hands, she placed the Paschal loaf with its gleaming red egg baked into it. "Today is Orthodox Easter, you see, because we don't celebrate on the same date that non-Orthodox do. This is special Easter bread. Christ is risen!"

With a bleary look from the bread to Evgenia, the beggar woman moved away from her, muttering under her breath, "Thank you. Thank you."

Couldn't she say anything but that? But what had Evgenia expected her to say? As long as she ate the bread and appreciated it, that would be enough.

Turning to go back into the bakery, Evgenia caught sight of a young Greek standing next to a car parked across the street, and as she recognized him, she felt hot blood rush to her cheeks. That particular young man, the one visiting from Greece whom she'd been longing to have look at her! For him to see her like this, without make-up or jewelry, her hair uncurled and barely brushed, and worse, to catch her giving Paschal bread away to beggars.

Well, I don't care if he did see, I'm not ashamed of being charitable for once in my life. If only that were wholly true, Evgenia reproached herself, but tossing her head, she retreated into the bakery.

But he was coming, the young man, crossing the street, and Evgenia fought down panic. "O Lord, help me! What if he talks to me?" If he came to the bakery door, should she open it or not? Should she pretend she hadn't seen him? If he had any sense at all, he must know she had seen him.

Nearing the bakery, he motioned for her to open the door, and she caught hold of it with all her strength, pulling it open, and faced him.

What a nice smile he had. "Evgenia Vasiliou, right?"

However did he know her name?

"My uncle Demetrios sent me over to pick you up for the lamb-feast, but I waited outside because I was early."

"Early? Greeks are never early," Evgenia stammered, and hated herself for saying something so stupid, that he might even consider insulting.

But he laughed. "This one was. Do you mind? When Demetrios said I was the only nephew he could spare to come and get you, I just came. If I hadn't, I wouldn't have seen you just now, and I wouldn't have wanted to miss that."

Maybe he was glad he'd seen so that he could laugh at her later. "It was silly."

With a glance down the street where the old beggar woman was hobbling away, her bread clutched close to her under her ragged shawl, he shook his head. "If I were that woman, I wouldn't think it was silly."

"But it was Paschal bread."

"What difference does that make? Today's Pascha, so it's all right." As he spoke, his smile danced into his eyes, warming Evgenia, reassuring her that he meant what he said, and that he wouldn't laugh at her. "Are you ready to go? The car's across the street."

Shooting pains spread out from Tamar's heart, so that she wobbled as she walked, but she clutched the bread. Greek Easter bread, the girl had said, and that was the girl who never gave Tamar even a penny. There she was explaining to Tamar about Pascha, but perhaps Tamar needed the explanation. Wrapped up in herself as she had been of late, she had almost forgotten to track the days; almost forgotten when Pascha fell this year.

Baked into the bread was a red egg, the symbol of life in Christ. Georgians, too, dyed eggs red for Pascha, to symbolize life. What sort of life did Tamar have, with no home but the streets of this poor section of the city? But the girl who had given her the bread was one of those rude young people whom Tamar despised, and yet in her heart she had found charity. In Tamar's heart she would find . . . what? Emptiness?

Yes. Yes, recently, although it hadn't always been there. Once Tamar had tried to live close to God, but lately God had abandoned her.

Or not. Perhaps He had sent her this Paschal bread by the hand of an unlikely messenger. Could it be possible that it was she who had gone away from God, and not He from her? How long had it been since she last prayed, she who in her youth had imagined herself pious? God, in His love, had left her her free will; left her free to turn her back on Him if she chose.

What had she done? Who did she think she was, complaining that she had no home, when the Son of Man Himself had had nowhere to lay His head? He had been a stranger in His own created world, and had been killed by His own people, and Tamar dared to complain to Him of her lot?

Bursting into bitter tears, she cried out in Georgian, "O God, forgive me, a sinner!"

Oh, how her chest hurt. Somewhere she must find a place to sit; perhaps there, in that alley, where the children who taunted her would be unlikely to find her. As old and sinful as she was, she must sit and pray.

Short of breath, full of pain, she lowered herself down to the ground next to a garbage can, and crouched there in the shadow of a wall, thinking of Pascha in Georgia, with bells ringing from all the churches in Tbilisi, and crowds with candles overflowing from the churches onto the streets, shouting, "Christ is risen!"

Truly He is risen. Truly, even here.

Closing her eyes, Tamar sucked in a deep breath full of the smells of gasoline and the filth in the alley where she sat. In the midst of all this, Christ was risen. For the sake of the world which had abandoned

Him, even for the sake of Tamar who had abandoned Him, Christ was risen. He was risen, and Hades was mocked and despoiled. Death held no terrors for a Christian who loved and feared and followed the risen Lord.

Death. Why did she think of death? Already she could hardly think at all around the pain spreading throughout her body, and her heart was a pulsing mass, fluttering and straining in her chest.

"O Lord God, help me!"

As she had always prayed in Georgian, so she prayed now in Georgian, begging for forgiveness and to draw closer to God before it was too late. With her last gasping breaths, she cried out to the Lord, knowing that He would hear her, hoping that He would take pity. Though she had gone away from Him, she had come back, and though she knew the multitude of her sins, she also knew His mercy. "Forgive me, forgive me, a sinner, for truly Thou art risen."

For truly He was, and she, repenting, dared to hope that He would grant her, even her, life and resurrection in Him.

In the midst of the babble of Greek and English, with the smoke of the roasting lamb drifting across the yard, carrying the warm smell of meat, Michael paused to glance up at the sun and blue sky that the Lord had made, and around at the people He had created: the priest discussing something with a parish councilor; the priest's wife in the midst of a group of women busy setting out food; Demetrios, the host, bustling between the lamb on its spit and the wine table; John the carpenter and John the construction worker arguing with much handwaving about something; Nikolia, still tired from the birth, showing off her baby to other young wives; Evgenia talking to Demetrios' nephew from Greece, the one who was reputed to be so particular about young women.

The Lord's creatures all, busy celebrating His Resurrection on this day that He had made; but Evgenia looked especially joyful, fresher and less adorned than usual, with a smile shining out of her eyes. As she looked, so Michael felt, light with holy joy; the Lord's gift to a man who might, in time, learn to be a man of prayer.

At home in the freezer, three extra loaves of prosphora waited to be needed, and however many loaves remained of Evgenia's Paschal bread waited to be sold in the bakery or given away as Paschal gifts.

The Day Christ Was Born

"What then is this bleating of sheep in my ears?
What is this lowing of cattle that I hear?"
But ask the animals, and they will teach you,
or the birds of the air, and they will tell you;
or speak to the earth, and it will teach you,
or let the fish of the sea inform you.

(I Sam.15:14, Job 12:7-8)

'Twas the eve of the thirteenth day after Christmas, and Evan had just arrived that day in Wales, after spending the entire twelve days of the holiday visiting his aunt and uncle in London. The bus had left him off at the village, and he had hiked the last two miles home on foot.

Now he paused to catch his breath for a moment, settling onto a grassy ridge above the valley. From here, his house was in view, nestled on the peak of a small hill at the other end of the valley. The night sky seemed very black compared to the orange glow that filled the streets of London at this hour, and Evan's eyes caught glimpses of pale stars burning far away overhead. It was chilly here, under them—his breath misted frostily before his face—and a wind ruffled under his anorak, making him shiver as he stood up and stretched his mittened hands.

"Christ is born!"

The voice floated to him on the wind, soft, yet full of joy. More voices joined in—who was there? No, it was only the wind. Evan looked closely at the patch of darkness in the valley. White shapes grazed there—it was late for the sheep to be away from their pens.

"Gwynn!" He whistled for the dog and started down to the valley to meet him.

Hurried paws came from his shed behind the house, and Evan heard him pant as he approached.

"Yes, sir? Are you wanting work tonight? On Christmas Eve?" The voice was low and gruff, and—and—it seemed to come from the dog.

Evan looked hard. "I'm dreaming . . ." he said, his voice trailing off as another chorus of "Christ is born" came from the direction of the sheep.

"Glorify Him!" cried Gwynn, running towards them.

Evan rubbed his forehead in dismay. *Am I crazy?* he thought. *It isn't even Christmas Eve, it's—*

"Evan, is that you?"

"Yes, Mum, I'm here!" He ran up the hill towards the open door where his mother stood framed in light and warmth.

She held out her arms to him. "Merry Christmas!"

"Merry Christmas to you, too, Mum!"

"Had a good holiday, did you?"

"Yes, Mum."

"And you're wearing your mittens, are you?"

"Yes, Mum."

"That's good. Come in and get heated up by the fire a bit."

"I'd like to. Where's Da?"

"Out to the barn."

"He's getting the sheep?"

She nodded.

"It's late for them," said Evan, the voices still running through his head, puzzling him.

"A bit late, but they'll do. Darkness never hurt a flock, and Gwynn's a good herder. Your Da'll get them all in pens all right."

"When's supper, Mum?" called Rhiannon from the stairs.

"Come down, child. It won't be long."

Evan sighed contentedly as he stuck his toes out by the fire, feeling them crinkle as they thawed. He would ask Da about the voices. No doubt they were in his head, but Da would know. His Da always knew.

They heard Da's heavy boots come in, and the wind whistled as he shut the back door against it.

"Twenty-eight sheep and none are black; shear 'em and graze 'em and put 'em back, put 'em back," he sang, pulling off his boots with a thwack and replacing them with slippers. He peeled off his jacket and came into the room, still singing under his breath.

Evan smiled up at him.

"Merry Christmas, stranger!" Da's big voice seemed to fill the room with cheer. "How's London—bustling, then?"

"Yes, of course. Aunt Jane never stopped complaining about the shopping."

"And my brother?"

"He sent you back a present, Da." Evan dug in the pockets of his anorak.

"Tobacco, I hope."

"Yes, that's it." He handed the packet to his father.

"There's Twinkle," purred Rhiannon, going on her knees and holding out one hand to the tabby. "Where's Gwynn, then?"

"Outside."

"But, Da, it's cold out there! He'll freeze!"

"Ah, leave him be, Rhi. He likes it."

She shook her head vehemently.

Evan laughed. "What do you know about it, Rhi? Maybe he does like it."

"You just want him frozen." She turned back to calling the cat, who was now busily washing herself.

"Supper's ready," said Mum. "Someone call Gwladys and Gwilym." She slipped into the other room to gently wake the sleeping baby, Alun.

The twins came down late, but Evan didn't even notice; nor did he notice what the supper meal was or the bit of it that he spilled on his shirt, for his mind was entirely occupied with puzzling over the voices outside. They had had an animal quality to them, and he remembered clearly being awake and alert at the time, yet . . .

"Pass the butter, Evan." Rhiannon jerked her elbow into his. "Daydreaming, is it?"

"Butter?—oh." He passed it to her, ignoring her tongue as she stuck it out rudely at him.

"Rhi, those aren't table manners, those," warned Da.

"Sorry." Her reply lacked repentance.

"It's so cold in here," said Gwladys.

"I was just thinking the same," said Gwilym.

"I'm hot," said Rhiannon.

"Well, you've got a back to the fire. Shall you switch places with Rhi and Evan, Gwilym and Gwladys?" said Mum.

"Aye." They got up simultaneously, moving to the other side of the table.

"Can I talk to you after supper, Da?" said Evan quietly, as he carried his napkin and plate to Gwilym's place.

"Aye." Da smiled at his son, whose dark hair framed a small but serious face.

Evan smiled back, suddenly reassured by his father's lively eyes. Surely his Da could reasonably explain what he had heard.

The baby began to wail in his high chair, and Mum took him onto her lap, rocking him softly in her arms.

Rhiannon slid into Gwladys's seat, smiling across at the twins, and they all fell to in silence.

"Come in, Evan." Da held the door open for his son.

Evan paused on the threshold. It was a rare pleasure to be invited into Da's tiny private study, and he gazed around at it in awe. The walls were dark and lined with bookcases that were crammed with books, and by the single window a desk and chair took up the remaining space.

"What's to talk about, then?" said Da, fiddling with the three-legged portable heater.

"Well, it sounds a bit odd."

"Yes?"

Evan nodded. "Something I heard. I was walking home from the bus stop, and I sat a moment on the hill to catch my breath."

"Then what?"

"I heard something in the valley—voices saying 'Christ is born.' I saw the sheep, too, and it was late for them. So I called for Gwynn, and—and he spoke to me. It was the voice I would imagine him having, but . . ."

"But what?"

"But he hasn't got any voice but for barking or growling!"

Da nodded thoughtfully. "Aye, well, legend has it that the animals talk on Christmas Eve."

"Christmas Eve! That was almost two weeks ago, Da!"

"It's not good enough, then? Come, sit on my knee. I've a story to tell."

Evan climbed onto his father's lap, frowning.

"When Jesus was born, 'twas the twenty-fifth of December according to the old calendar from long ago. Later, someone made up a new calendar. But a few really traditional people decided not to follow it— they wanted to stick with the old calendar that had been used for so many centuries. Those few say that Christmas is really thirteen days later than the December twenty-fifth of our calendar."

"Thirteen days . . ."

"Aye, so that makes it Christmas Eve tonight."

"Then why don't we have Christmas tomorrow—January seventh— if that's the real day?"

Da shrugged. "Modernization. It's not important really—no one knows for sure when Jesus Christ was born, and besides there's no time but what mankind has made up."

"But, Da, I heard the animals, and they wouldn't make a mistake— would they?"

"I don't know, Evan. I just know that things change, and we've got to change with them or we'll get left behind, see?"

"Why?"

"Well, you'll understand when you're grown up, my boy." Da glanced at his watch. "You ought to get to bed now, Evan. 'Tis past time."

"All right. Good night." He kissed his father, then left the study and hurried upstairs. It was the first thing his Da had ever said that didn't make sense. The animals wouldn't make a mistake. But if this were really Christmas Eve, then the Christmas he had always known wasn't Christmas at all, just a date chosen by someone, on which nothing out-of-the-ordinary had ever happened!

Evan got ready for bed as fast as he could in the chilliness, then went to the window and pushed it up high. Below him, the stable stuck out from the back of the house, lending it warmth and sometimes odor. He leaned out into the air over it, cocking his head and listening. From far away came a faint murmur of the wind across the grassy land, and it blew a soft but icy blast into his face.

At last he heard them—the quietly bleating voices of the sheep mixed with the slightly lower voices of the cow and the dog. They seemed to be beginning a hymn; and as the words floated up, Evan hastily wrote them down on a scrap of paper:

"Thy nativity, O Christ our God, hath shined the light of knowledge upon the world; for thereby they that worshipped the stars were instructed by a star to worship Thee, the Sun of Righteousness, and to know Thee, the Dayspring from on high. O Lord, glory be to Thee."

There was a knock on the door just as he finished scribbling, and Evan crawled into bed and pulled the covers up to his chin. "Come in!"

"Evan, where's my boy?"

"Oh, Mum. I've gone to bed."

She came in and kissed his forehead. "Brr. The cold is bad in here. Why, what's this? The window's flung wide!" Mum slammed it shut. "You'll catch your death to sleep with the frost coming in, Evan."

"Yes, Mum."

"Really, I mean it."

"I was about to shut the window, but—"

"Don't open it again, dearie, on such a cold day. It cools out the whole house, then." She went to the door. "Goodnight, Evan."

"Goodnight, Mum. Merry Christmas."

She laughed. "Merry Christmas."

Then the door shut behind her with a swish.

She probably doesn't know what day it is tomorrow, he thought. *No one does but Da, and he doesn't care. He doesn't even care that all his life he's been celebrating on the wrong day!—and so have I, but I'll try to remember the Christ Child tomorrow.*

He laid the pen and paper with the hymn on it on the shelf by his bed and turned over on his side, with his dark head against the pillow.

"Happy Birthday, Baby Jesus," he whispered in the darkness.

"A present?" said Mum, smiling. "What for?"

It was on the tip of his tongue to say why, but Evan only smiled back. "It's nothing much."

She tore open the paper. "A seashell! How lovely, darling! You're so sweet." She gave him a hug and kiss.

Evan kept on smiling, thinking of the Christ Child. It had been worth it to give up his treasured seashell in order to celebrate the real Christmas.

"Now he's going to ask for something, Mum," said Rhiannon, swinging fast in the rocking chair and sucking on a lollipop.

"Rhi, that's cruel," said Gwladys, then she cried out in pain as she stuck her finger with her embroidery needle.

Alun gurgled happily, sharing Gwilym's lap with the cat Twinkle.

"Oh, there's Gwynn." Rhiannon leaped off the rocking chair, letting it teeter violently on its rockers, as the dog padded in from outside.

Da entered behind him, his cheeks rosy from the cold. "I met Dafydd Jones outside Rhodri's Drugstore."

"Aye? How's the old man, then?" said Mum, frowning at Rhiannon, who had hit Evan for petting Gwynn's shaggy ears when she wanted to. Gwynn's eyes reproached her, and he lay down with both paws over Evan's hand.

Da came in by the fire and took up the paper. "Fit as a fiddle, he is.

He was off to that church of his this morning and wished me a merry Christmas."

She chuckled. "Never would let go of the old ways, he."

"He's got the blood of the ancient saints in him, I'm thinking," agreed Da.

"No more people like that, now, for certain. And he still calls that old stone building 'church,' then?"

"Aye. 'Tis a ruin, but he won't go elsewhere." Da sighed. "Well, he won't last much longer, now, for all he's so spry and bright-eyed. How long has it been? Sixty, seventy years that he's lived up on the peak?"

"About that."

They went on talking, and no one noticed that Evan had slipped to the back of the house. He put his boots on as quietly as he could, then wrapped a scarf around his neck, a hat over his head, pulled on thick gloves, and went outside.

A silvery hoarfrost coated the ground; it crunched under his feet as he hurried down the hill. A noise made him look back, and he saw Gwynn running after him. Evan waited for the dog to catch up, then they went on together.

He knew where to go—why had he not thought of it before? Dafydd Jones was always coming from or going to the stone building in the trees.

"Come on, Gwynn, we're nearly there!"

The dog caught the tremor of excitement in Evan's voice and ran ahead of him towards the fringe of trees that crowded round a small building that remained sacred to the people of the Old Church. Dafydd was the last of them, and he alone could not keep it up, so the church had fallen into disrepair. Yet even with the moss and weeds that wound around its crumbling stones, something about the mellowed gray walls seemed to offer peace and shelter to all God's people.

Evan slipped noiselessly inside, pulling off his hat as he did so, but Gwynn settled respectfully in the grass at the doorstep.

It was a small, shadowy room that smelled sweet, as if the fragrance of incense from ages past remained trapped in its enclosed walls. A row of dark wooden benches lined the northern side, and facing east stood a stone structure which separated the nave from the altar and formed an open archway in the center.

Evan caught sight of Dafydd Jones standing in the dim light of one of the windows, holding his woolen cap and a candle in one hand and crossing himself with the other as he muttered prayers.

He was a small man, with a face as worn as a rock that the wind had beat upon for many years; but whenever he spoke, his words were gentle and full of wisdom.

Evan tried making the sign of the cross too—for the first time—imagining the small room crammed with people and full of light. He wondered why it felt holier than the church his family went to every feast-day. Perhaps because it held a remembrance of a past time full of glorious saints who had willingly denied themselves for God. Perhaps because it hadn't chosen to follow "modernization" over truth.

He pulled a slip of paper from his pocket and read to himself the words he had heard the animals sing.

"Christ is born," said a voice beside him.

"Yes, He—He is." Evan found Dafydd's eyes upon him.

"Who are you, child?"

"I'm Evan Morgan—you know, Madoc's son."

"I see." Dafydd stood smiling for a moment, then spoke again. "Do you know what day it is, Evan Morgan?"

"Yes, sir. It's Christmas Day, but no one else believes it."

Dafydd chuckled, and his face became a thousand merry wrinkles. "Who's taught you, child? Surely not Madoc!"

"It was the animals, sir."

Evan clutched his hymn tightly, wanting to show the old man, yet not wanting to give up his new secret treasure.

"I've a hymn," he said at last.

"From your head?"

"No, from the animals. They were speaking."

Dafydd nodded, holding the candle up to it. Taking the paper, the old man read the words under his breath. "How beautiful. Glory to God," he said. "but you know that it's just you and me left now? What did Madoc name ye?"

"I'm Evan Morgan."

"Oh, aye, you told me before." He smiled at his own forgetfulness. "You must be a better child than most—no other would have come here today, even if he did hear the animals on Christmas Eve."

Evan shook his head. "No, I'm no better than most."

"Well, well." Dafydd sank onto a bench with a whistling sigh, and Evan sat down beside him, wondering at how odd he felt. No presents, no stocking, no tree, no cookies, no candy, not even a service to make it feel like Christmas, yet somehow the true spirit of the feast was in him—it was a spirit he had never known.

"Will you come to my hut, Evan Morgan?" said Dafydd, rising from the bench. "I have tea and Christmas cookies from my sister."

"They'll miss me at home, I'm afraid."

"Aye?" The old man sounded wistful, and suddenly it occurred to Evan that perhaps he missed company all alone on the peak, where he lived.

"But I'll come anyhow. Do you like dogs?"

"Any creature of God's is welcome in my home. Where's your dog?"

They went to the door, then stepped out into the brisk wintry air. Gwynn got up, wagging his tail and looking like he was thoroughly tired of sitting in the cold.

"Here he is." Evan ruffled the fur around the dog's neck.

"A charming chap. Does he have a name, then?"

"Gwynn."

"Well, come with us, Gwynn. I'll see if I haven't got something you'd like for eating at the hut, too." Dafydd put his woolen cap on his head, then turned directly towards the hills, walking very fast. Evan and Gwynn hurried to follow his flapping overcoat.

"Nice clear sort of day."

"I'm cold," said Evan.

"Tsk, tsk, where's your endurance?"

"I'm low on it in winter."

"Aye, we're all low on it, child. I was only teasing you, then." He looked back with a smile.

They continued for a while in silence, until at last the hut came into view. It seemed a long way up, but the slope carried them so gently that in no time they had reached it. Evan paused to look down at the countryside spread out before him.

"Come in, come in, it's lots warmer inside—or will be, once the fire's going, then."

Inside, the hut was dry and clean. "But no one's allowed upstairs," said Dafydd, with a laugh. "That's where the mess is." He shook his head as if his clutter were hopeless.

"Can I help with something?"

"See, there, I knew you were an unusual child. Here, help me get a good stack of logs piled in the fireplace. We're wanting a lovely blaze for Christmas."

Evan threw the logs on and lit them, while Dafydd set the table and got out a large jar of cookies.

"My sister's always sending more," he said, piling them onto Evan's napkin. "She loves to cook and does it so well! Try the ones dipped in chocolate—that's the traditional kind. She's never passed a year without making me those ones."

"Mmmm, I like them." Evan licked his fingers. "What did you give Gwynn?"

"Oh, a bit of meat pasty I got at Rhodri's yesterday."

Evan nodded. "He likes that sort of thing, if you don't mind giving it to him."

The old man shrugged. "Why not? It's Christmas!"

"Where've you been, Evan?" Rhi frowned as he came in the back door with red cheeks and nose.

"Out—it's no business of yours."

Her nose shot up into the air. "Well, you missed tea, and Mum was wanting you."

"Is Evan back, then?" called Mum.

"Yes, I'm here." He knelt to untie his boots and pull the heavy mittens from his hands.

"I was wanting you for helping your Da."

"Aye? Where is he?"

"Mucking out the barn. Gwilym's gone to help a bit, but he grumbled about it."

"Well, I'll go." He hastily tied up his boots again and slipped back outside.

"Come to help at last, eh?" said Gwilym, who was on his knees scrubbing out the cow's trough, while Da raked up the old straw on the dirt floors.

"Get the bundle, there, Evan," said Da, pointing to a heap of fresh, clean straw propped against the wall. "I want it sprinkled after me, wherever I've raked."

"All right." Evan untied the bundle and began the work.

"Is this good enough, Da?" Gwilym stood up and stretched, looking like he would rather be anywhere else.

"Oh, it'll do."

"Good. I've been wanting a ride on my motor-bike. Where've you stowed it?"

"In the shed until we've finished cleaning." Da sighed as his eldest son went outside. "I wish he'd be more of a help, that boy."

Evan was silent.

"Well, and where were you?" said Da, after a few moments.

"Nowhere special. I'm always off somewhere and you don't much care."

"But I know it's got to do with yesterday night."

Evan shrugged. "What if it does?"

"Off to church, was it?"

"Yes, Da. I met Dafydd Jones there."

"Listen, son, I don't mind you being religious, but why don't you just stick with what everyone else does, eh?"

"No, Da. It's not right."

"Am I wrong, then?"

"I don't know." Evan looked at the ground, where the freshly-strewn straw lay like a neat carpet.

"It's not doing harm to have Christmas on one day instead of another, and that way we fit in, then. See how I mean, Evan?"

"I see, but—I—I think it does matter."

Da shrugged. "Do what you want, then, but don't ask the rest of us to change our ways."

"No, Da, I won't."

Both continued the work in silence.

"There's the supper bell," said Da, after what seemed like ages.

They heard Gwilym's motor-bike putter to a stop outside, and he flung open the barn door. "Finished, Da?"

"Aye, bring in the machine, if you must."

Evan pulled off his hat and wiped his hot forehead with his hand. "I'm tired. Can I go now?"

"Yes, go on." Da, too, prepared to leave, tidying everything before he went.

Inside, Mum was bustling about. "Supper's on the table!" she called out the door, as Da and Gwilym appeared from the barn.

"I had a good ride around the hills," said Gwilym. "But I'll be needing some money, Da, for a check-up on the bike."

"'Needing?'" repeated Mum. She looked at her husband. "Only if the budget will allow it."

They washed their hands and sat down to eat.

"This is my favorite meal," said Rhiannon, holding a forkful to her nose with a deep sniff.

Mum laughed. "That's good to hear, that is."

When all had been cleared away at last, Evan went up to his room. Against Mum's wishes, he flung the window wide. He put his hand out and felt the softness of falling snow. "Happy Birthday, Lord," he said into the night, "and thank you for the merry Christmas."

Then, from somewhere in the darkness, Evan heard a shepherd whistling to call his sheep, and it made him think of how the animals had shown him the true Christmas day, and how the Good Shepherd had called him to His fold.

The Novice

Sister Nectaria yawned as she reached the top of the stairs, and as she turned, her eyes met the picture again—the one that annoyed her every time she saw it. It was a portrait of Paraskevi, smiling, her black hair arranged perfectly under a white scarf and the fringe of the scarf draped artistically over her shoulder. Her high-necked dress with its flowing silk sleeves was painted dark crimson. Around her neck hung a large, shining cross. She looked like a woman who was used to riches and happiness, and Sister Nectaria resented that.

She herself had been born poor and alone in the world except for her sickly mother. All that she had wished for in life had been denied her, and the only place where she had found peace and joy had been at the Convent of the Dormition. But now, as a novice at that convent, she was constantly tempted by the evil one, who worked hard to destroy that peace and joy and to interrupt her as she prayed. It was unfair. All her life she had struggled, and her mother's death had left her in utter poverty, physically and mentally. The convent had been her one refuge, and now she took her place there, yet seemed to be only a shadow among the nuns. She felt that life had slammed its heavy doors in her face, and she was to be forever on the outside looking in.

So she envied Paraskevi, the woman whom everyone spoke of as someone special. Although Sister Nectaria had never seen her in person, she knew that she was indeed as rich as she appeared in her portrait, for she gave large donations to the convent—even if she never came to church—and she was a favorite of the Abbess, Mother Angeliki. She seemed to have everything in life, while Sister Nectaria had nothing.

"Keep praying to God," Mother Angeliki had told her. "He will show you if the monastic life is His will for you or not. Just be patient." Perhaps in this way the Abbess meant to warn her that she was not making a good start as a novice. Well, it was true, and many times she had thought of leaving the convent.

"You forgot to sweep the kitchen floor," said Mother Marcella, coming up behind her.

"Oh, I'm sorry."

Mother Marcella disappeared down the hall, and Sister Nectaria went back downstairs and into the kitchen. No one else was around but meek and quiet Sister Photini, still putting away the dinner dishes, which should have been done before the vigil.

Sister Nectaria got out the broom and began sweeping. It was summer, and even though the hot sun had set long ago, she perspired under her mandelia. The floor seemed to have grown and spread out, covering a huge distance; by the time she had finally finished sweeping it, Sister Photini was gone, and Sister Nectaria felt ready to collapse. She poured herself some water and ate a snack in the trapeza, then went back upstairs, this time by way of the back passage, which didn't lead her past Paraskevi's portrait.

As she entered her cell, the clock in the hall struck quarter of one. At first she didn't think about what that meant, but then she realized that it was already Sunday morning and she had just eaten a snack. They were only allowed to eat until midnight, and she had gotten a blessing for a snack hours ago but put off eating it, forgetting the time. Now she couldn't receive Communion tomorrow.

Sister Nectaria sank onto her bed with a sigh, feeling as if she wanted to cry, but she was too tired to do so. She crossed herself and pulled her prayer-rope from her pocket, then got to her feet and tried to pray. Her mind wandered, and she yawned again and again.

At last she got into bed; and as her head touched the pillow, she fell asleep.

Sister Nectaria had read half of her Communion Prayers the next morning before she remembered about her snack. She put the book down, almost with relief, for she heard the nuns downstairs already finishing the Doxology. She flung on her rasa and veil and hurried to the church.

As she kissed Mother Angeliki's hand, she caught the shadow of a look that reproached her for being late. Sister Nectaria bent her head and went to her place. As she stood there, still with her head down, a sudden wave of self-pity came over her. She had never enjoyed a life of pleasure as had Paraskevi, yet when she came and labored endlessly as a novice, her abbess still preferred rich and smiling Paraskevi. What a cheerful woman she was, the nuns always said. But Sister Nectaria had no reason to be cheerful. She tried to fit in with the other nuns and novices, but no one seemed to appreciate her.

Father Stephanos had insisted that Mother Calliope use his favorite incense in the hand censer again, even though it bothered everyone's throat but his. As the choir began the Thrice-Holy Hymn, and Mother Calliope censed the iconostasis, the nuns interrupted their singing with coughs.

Sister Nectaria coughed, too, and her voice was so loud at one point that the deacon turned around and looked at her.

She hurried out of the church, her throat still scratchy, and in her rush she dropped her prayer-rope on the floor.

But the front hall wasn't free of incense smoke either, so her coughing didn't stop right away. In the midst of it, she realized that her prayer-rope was missing, and she cleared her throat and walked back to the church to see if it might be on the bench.

Sister Nectaria almost stepped on it before she saw it lying black against the pale rug. She bent down, picked it up, and went back to her place, feeling glad for once that she could so easily fade in among the other dark-clothed figures.

After Communion, she and the other novices had to leave the service early to dish up the meal, which today was an unappetizing soup served with paximadi.

"Do we have dessert?" she asked Sister Photini.

"I don't know. Ask Sister Theodosia."

Sister Theodosia was too busy to pay any attention to her until she had asked three times about dessert. Then she said quickly, "Mother Marcella said to put out the phinikia Paraskevi gave us."

Sister Nectaria took the big box of cookies and put one at each place.

"Can you pour the water?" said Sister Theodosia, coming from the kitchen with a special bowl of soup for Mother Angeliki.

"But I'm not done with the dessert."

"Well, I want you to pour the water now."

Sister Nectaria put the cookies down and began filling up the glasses.

As usual, they finished getting everything ready just as Mother Angeliki and the other nuns filed into the trapeza singing. Everyone stood behind their chairs. Then Father Stephanos blessed the food, they sat down, and one of the nuns began to read the life of Saint Christina, whose feast it was that day.

When the food was cleared away, the table wiped off, and Sister Photini was washing the dishes, Sister Nectaria got a blessing to go down to the garden to sit in the shade for a while and rest.

There was a little breeze that ruffled her mandelia, and the heat wasn't so stifling under the tree where she sat. From above her came the cheery voice of a cardinal.

"Sister Nectaria?" Someone was hurrying towards her from the hill, and it looked like Sister Theodosia.

"What is it?"

Sister Theodosia paused to catch her breath. "I've been looking all over for you; Mother Juliana doesn't feel well, so you're on duty now."

"Oh." Sister Nectaria stood up reluctantly. "I hope she feels better soon," she said stiffly.

The two novices went back up to the house, and Mother Marcella met them inside.

"Sister Theodosia, Mother Angeliki wants to see you for a minute," she said.

"All right."

They left Sister Nectaria alone in the hall, and as she pulled out her prayer-rope wool, she thought how much she dreaded being on duty. They knew it, too, but she still had to do it because she was only a novice. They expected her to obey, even when she didn't want to.

She got out the prayer-rope that she was slowly making. It was dark gray wool with olivewood beads from the Holy Land. She crossed herself and tried to focus on saying the Jesus Prayer; then she began making knots, praying at the same time that no one would call or come to the door. Her fingers snarled up the wool, but she kept on going, anxious to finish the prayer-rope because she rarely found time to work on it at all.

Sister Nectaria had made six knots when the clock struck twelve and the doorbell rang simultaneously. Setting the prayer-rope on the hall table, she got up, and opened the door.

"Thank you," said the woman outside, smiling at her as she wheeled herself in.

Sister Nectaria looked at her in astonishment. It was surely Paraskevi—she could see that from the woman's face and from the white, fringed scarf over her black hair—but she was in a wheelchair!

"What is your name?" asked the woman.

"Sister Nectaria."

"I'm Paraskevi Spiridakis."

"Yes, I recognize you from your portrait. But—what happened...?"

"Oh, you mean . . . I had polio when I was a child."

"I'm sorry," said Sister Nectaria.

Paraskevi smiled. "That's all right," she said. "But I'd like to go into the church. Can you get me some candles, Sister Nectaria?" She handed the novice several dollars.

Sister Nectaria nodded, still overcome by surprise, and went to get the candles.

Once inside the church, Paraskevi crossed herself and bent her head, and Sister Nectaria saw that her cheerful smile had been replaced by a look of sober compunction. Her lips moved in prayer and she kept making the sign of the cross until tears began to flow silently down her cheeks.

Sister Nectaria stood motionless, ashamed. Here a woman in a wheelchair humbly cried out to God, while she herself—a novice for Him—couldn't utter a prayer that wasn't tinged with bitterness and self-pity. Paraskevi did not to have the perfect life that Sister Nectaria had envisioned her with, yet she had a faith that sustained her even through all of her physical sufferings.

"Sister Nectaria, will you put these on the candlestand for me?" she asked, her face now washed over with a peaceful light.

"Of course."

Paraskevi smiled again at Sister Nectaria. "Thank you so much," she said. "I don't come to church often because my legs bother me so much, but today I just wanted to see it. You are so lucky to have this chapel, my dear. I've always wanted to be a nun, but I'm not physically strong enough." She smiled again.

"Oh, will you please pray for me?" Sister Nectaria blurted out all at once, as her own eyes threatened to overflow with tears.

Paraskevi nodded. "And you pray for me too. Pray especially that I'll make it to Liturgy for my nameday on Tuesday."

"I will," said Sister Nectaria.

Paraskevi turned towards the door. "Oh, I almost forgot," she said, taking a letter from her pocket. "Don't disturb her now, but this is for Mother Angeliki."

"She'll be sorry to have missed seeing you," said Sister Nectaria.

"I'll be back again soon, God willing. Thank you for helping me in the church, my dear."

"Oh, you're welcome."

Sister Nectaria opened the door for her, and Paraskevi crossed herself as she went over the threshold.

"Do you need some help getting in the car?"

"Oh, no, my sister Maria is there waiting for me. You know, she doesn't like to come in because she's New Calendar, but she doesn't mind carting me around. Good-bye, Sister Nectaria," she said, turning to her with a smile as she wheeled away.

"Good-bye."

Sister Nectaria went back inside and shut the door, then she sat down and picked up the prayer-rope again. Somehow, now, the gray yarn slipped smoothly into beautiful knots that she would have looked at with selfish pride had she not known that their beauty came not from her fingers, but from God. She would never forget how she had judged Paraskevi so wrongly, yet God had used that sin to bring her to humility.

The Hospitality
of the British

A damp chill had come over the sea and settled on the land. In the north and west, snow coated the highlands and the unsettled mountains, becoming mist that promised rain as it descended to the lower regions of the south and east. A lone traveler, his cloak wrapped around his head and shoulders, trudged down a paved road, stopping from time to time to straighten and raise his hand to his eyes, scanning the land. In the far distance, half-seen through the mist and the fading light, he spotted the round wall of a homestead, with a trickle of smoke drifting up from the round British house of wattle and daub within the enclosure. Grimacing, the traveler stepped off the road into the tall wet grass, pausing at a grove of oaks to cut himself a staff.

The Roman legions that had once subdued and civilized the native Britons were seventy-five years gone, leaving a heritage of roads, towns, Christian churches, villas, retired legionaries, and a memory of more prosperous times, before the first Scots raided the land from Ireland or the first Anglo-Saxons from Germany. Years of civil strife had beaten down the Britons, while their leaders quarreled with each other and hired Anglo-Saxon mercenaries, who called themselves *foederati* or treaty troops, to help them drive off the Anglo-Saxon raiders. As often as not, the *foederati* turned against their paymasters, taking by force the British land that would have been their wages. And the pagan Irish and Anglo-Saxon barbarians continued to raid.

One British leader had risen against them, striving to make Britain safe and free again, and now another man followed in his footsteps, placating the petty chieftains and rousing the Britons to fight for him and for their land. But already the Anglo-Saxon grip on the southern and eastern coastlands had grown too strong to shake off.

Hidden in the damp gray mist, the lowlands brooded. Within the walls of his round house, Rhys ab Ewein, a short and stocky Briton with shaggy dark hair and a drooping mustache, lounged before the fire, his evening work left undone but for the feeding of his sheep on

43

this evening before the Nativity feast. Seated at his feet, his oldest daughter wove a melody for the Christ Child on her harp, and his two young sons, lingering over a game of *gwyddbwyll* *, glanced at each other, grinned, and raised their voices in harmony. After a moment their mother joined her voice to theirs from where she sat beside Rhys to tend the winter apples baking in the glowing cinders.

The tall, hawk-faced man crouching before the fire glanced up at Rhys. "Before God, she plays like one endowed with a gift from on high."

Rhys inclined his head. "You do her honor, Meilic ap Taran."

"She does herself honor." Meilic rose from before the fire, giving his place to his own harp, careful not to touch the strings and disturb the girl's song.

"You'll sing for us after dinner, won't you?"

"If it pleases you."

Rhys smiled. "It pleases us all. It isn't every night that we offer hospitality to a prince's bard."

Meilic's reluctant smile flitted across his lips. "You play on my vanity, Rhys."

"And you on your harp."

They both started at the sound of rough pounding on the door. The girl's song died in a discordant twang of harpstrings. Rhys jumped to his feet. "Not a friend, or he would have walked in. A stranger." He went to the door.

In the darkness outside stood a man wrapped in dark wool, holding a staff in his hand. Taking him for a monk, Rhys pulled the door wide open and stood aside. "Come in and be welcome! It's a cold night for traveling, that's certain. Please, honor my house. Come in, eat with us, spend the night, and come with us to church for the feast tomorrow."

The man stepped in, letting Rhys close the door and shut off the cold draught.

"Warm yourself by the fire. Cadell, bring water to wash our guest's feet." Rhys motioned to one of his sons.

---

* A Welsh game similar to chess.

Laying aside his staff, the stranger crossed the room and knelt by the fire, his back to them. Rhys's daughter, with a glance at her father, resumed her song.

Little by little the stranger's hands regained their color, and at last he rose and, turning to Rhys, unwound his cloak from his head and let it fall with a whisper of wool to the floor. The face he uncovered was Anglo-Saxon, hidden in blond beard to the ears, his uncombed hair blond and silky, his eyes as blue as the depths of a mountain lake.

Rhys recoiled, his hand flying to the place on his belt where his knife should have hung, before he remembered himself and forced his hand to his side. The harpsong faltered and stopped. Rhys's wife smothered a cry.

The stranger met Rhys's eyes. "Don't be afraid." He spoke good British, but with a harsh accent.

Rhys gave him a level stare. "Are you a raider or one of the *foederati*?"

"*Foederati*." The stranger spread his hands. "Forgive me. In this cold, I feared never to wake if I spent the night outside."

Meilic stepped to Rhys's side, exchanging glances with him, but the bard didn't say what Rhys already knew. By the sacred law of hospitality, this Saxon, once invited in and offered water to wash his feet, became a guest, and Rhys would answer for any harm that came to him.

Rhys motioned to Cadell, who stood shifting from foot to foot with the bowl of water in his hands. "Wash our guest's feet."

The stranger let out his held breath. "I thank you."

Before they ate, Rhys's oldest daughter went to wake the two younger girls and bring them closer to the fire. Their eyes full of sleep, they clung to her as she set them beside her. Rhys's wife served the baked winter apples and a thick porridge of oatmeal on thin bread.

They sat in threes, Rhys's three daughters, his two sons and Meilic ap Taran, the Saxon alone until Rhys and his wife had seen that there was enough food for everyone. The meal passed in silence. After it, Meilic touched his harp and raised his eyebrows, and Rhys nodded, but he found it hard to think of the harpsong with the Saxon, pale and blond, sitting beside him. No one sang harmony. After two songs, Meilic set his harp aside.

Rhys rose. "We should sleep. Tomorrow we rise early for church."

The Saxon also stood up. "I shall leave before sunrise."

Scooping up the two younger girls, Rhys's wife carried them to the sleeping corner, motioning the Saxon to follow her. Meilic turned to the fire, waiting until Rhys came and knelt to bank it for the night. "Will you let him sleep here in peace, Rhys ab Ewein?"

"Yes."

"Then you have more trust for an untrustworthy race than many men I've met."

"No." Rhys stared down at the glowing coals. "No. I refuse to betray my guest."

When the others had fallen asleep, Rhys took his knife and laid it beside his seat by the banked fire. For most of the night he sat there, watching while the dark-haired Celts and the blond Saxon slept. Towards morning he picked up his daughter's harp and set his no-longer-accustomed fingers to the strings, calling forth the same song of the Christ Child that she had played the night before.

As if the song had summoned him, the Saxon came from the shadows of the hut to Rhys's side, seating himself cross-legged on the floor to listen in silence until Rhys stilled the strings.

"You play well." The man's Saxon accent harshened his words.

"Not as well as my daughter or Meilic ap Taran, but today is one of the most important feasts for Christians, the birth of our Saviour, and I wanted to play a song of joy."

"I learned one such from a British comrade-in-arms. Shall I play it for you?"

With some misgivings, Rhys handed him the harp.

Under the Saxon's touch, joyful music flowed from the strings, and as it filled the house, his travel-stained clothes turned blinding white and his face shone. With a cry, Rhys flung his arm across his eyes. The music soared to heaven, and a multitude of voices joined in the song.

As the echoes faded, Rhys heard the stranger rise and say in a quiet voice with no accent, "Fear not. I am leaving as I said I would, before your family wakes, and this house will be blessed for the hospitality of its master."

When he had gone, Rhys uncovered his eyes and stared, shaking, at the now-silent harp. "Praise God for preserving me from breaking the law of hospitality! For this night I have sheltered, unknowing, an angel of the Lord under my roof."

He seemed to hear in his soul the echoes of the angel's joyous hymn.

The Empty Church

One more hour. Bundled up for warmth, with a heavy scarf over her head and her mittened hands tucked in her coat-pockets, Ludmila Pavlova decided not to close early, much as she wanted to. Not, she reflected glumly, that any tourists would come by in the last hour before closing, and probably not any townspeople. Why not close early?

But if she did, what did she have to go home to? An empty house, inhabited only by memories: her husband, dead twelve years; the daughter who now lived in Moscow.

Ludmila stepped inside the church, glancing around in the fading light. She knew every step of the place, from the bare iconostasis at the front, to the historical exhibit along one white-washed wall, to the empty prince's tomb at the back. The Church of the Holy Theophany, it had once been called, in celebration of the Saviour's baptism by John in the Jordan. Once Russia, too, had been baptized, under Vladimir . . . but that was long ago. These days the church was a sight for tourists to come and stare at while Ludmila, after charging them an admission price five times higher than for locals, watched to make sure they didn't take pictures. Locals came too, sometimes, but mostly the tourists did, with their loud voices and their American jeans. Women, too, in jeans like the men.

And for sitting at the church door all day, and for keeping her eyes open when visitors came, Ludmila earned a pitiful salary, just enough for food.

In the growing dark, the church had become black as night inside, though the west still glowed pink, turning the snow rosy. Sighing, Ludmila stepped back outside, seating herself with a creak of aging bones in her chair beside the door.

At the end of every day her feet hurt more than the day before. Every day—especially in winter—she wanted to close early, but she hadn't done it yet.

She leaned her head back against the doorpost, clenching her hands inside her mittens. Last winter she'd had a heater, but it had broken, and she didn't have enough money for a new one. Asking her superiors for one would only cause trouble for her. During the day the cold was endurable, but after sunset sometimes she wondered if she would freeze to death.

One more reason to close early.

A last shaft of light slanted through a narrow window to shine on the iconostasis in the church, staining it red. Ludmila, squinting at it from her seat by the doorstep, imagined the red was the maroon of the Mother of God's clothing as it must have looked in the icon that had once hung where the light now shone. An icon of the Saviour would have hung where the light didn't reach, across from the Mother of God's icon, with the royal doors between. Priests in vestments of rich brocade would have served in the church, and the faithful would have come from the town. Once in a while a pilgrim might pass through, stopping to venerate the icons in the church. How many years ago had it all stopped? How had Russia, in less than a century, turned from a Christian land to a country full of derelict churches? Where had the grace of its baptism gone? How had Russia cast it away so quickly?

The old piety had died with Ludmila's mother's generation. Today's young people, like her daughter, looked forward to a new Russia, with a new god: money. If some went to church, most did it to be in style.

The crunch of feet from the snow-covered path to the church startled Ludmila. Gripping the door, she climbed to her feet. Had the hour passed yet? Could she close now?

In the new darkness, the moon appeared, shedding pale light over the church, Ludmila, and a stranger who had stopped on the path. Seeing Ludmila, he walked forward, saying, "May I go in?"

"Closed," she was about to snap, taking him for a tourist despite his Russian—or because of it, with the foreign accent that distorted it—but something about him made her hesitate. "600 rubles," she said instead, charging him only three times more than she would charge a local.

He paid and went in, wandering around the church, squinting at everything in the moonlight. Folding her arms over her chest, Ludmila stood and watched him. He wore a long coat, but sticking out from it she could see the legs of his jeans. An American, probably. No camera, though, that she saw, unless he wore it under his coat.

His inspection done, he turned to her. "I was hoping there'd be a service here tomorrow, but I guess there won't be, will there?"

"Young man, there hasn't been a service here since 1917."

"Oh. Are any of the churches in this town open?"

"They're all open." Ludmila knew what he meant, but she let him think she didn't in the hopes that he'd give up on her and leave. It was past closing time, and he had seen all there was to see. Why was he staying?

"If they're all as open as this one, there won't be services in any of them tomorrow."

He'd understood her. She almost wished he hadn't. "Why should there be? Tomorrow's not Sunday."

He gave her a wide American stare. "No, but it's the Theophany."

The Theophany? Oh, yes. It had been twelve days since Christmas, hadn't it? Ludmila felt a surge of shame. Here she sat lamenting the old piety, while she herself, going along day by day with nothing to do but the same things every day, lost track of the feasts. He was right, this young American. Tomorrow would be the nineteenth of January.

On the heels of that thought came a question that she asked before she considered it. "How did you know?"

"I've known for years, since I became Orthodox. I was afraid when I signed up for this trip that I'd miss services, but it was the only time I could go. I can't take the bus to Moscow, can I? No, I probably couldn't figure out how to do it anyway." Sighing, he glanced at her, his disappointment clear on his face. "Oh, well." His hand came out towards her, with something in a gold frame lying on his palm. "I'd like you to have this. I'm sorry if I kept you past closing time."

As the young man walked away, Ludmila raised the thing he had given her to the moonlight and saw that it was an icon of the Saviour receiving baptism. A lump rose in her throat. After all the things she had just been thinking about young people, and all the things she'd always believed about Americans, here a young American had given an icon to her. To her, Ludmila Pavlova, who worked at a church and forgot the Theophany. And he hadn't even known that was the church's feastday.

With the icon still in her hand, Ludmila stepped into the church to check that all was well, as she always did before locking up. Through the window shone a shaft of moonlight, lighting the bare iconostasis. Struck by an idea, Ludmila stepped up to the royal doors, rising on her toes and stretching her arm up as far as she could to fix the American's icon over the doors.

Then she stepped back. The presence of an icon, even one, made the church feel like a church again, not like an old building falling to ruin. Ludmila stood for a moment where the congregation would have stood in Christian Russia. How many years had it been since the last service in this church was held?

Yet, while once-Orthodox Christian Russia groaned under the Communist yoke, Orthodox people had been living in America, a land that had never been Orthodox. It had taken an American to restore Ludmila's hope. Even if Russia never regained its faith, there were Orthodox in America, where the money-god had been worshipped for far longer. True belief had not died with Ludmila's mother's generation. The grace conferred by Orthodox Baptism was still in the world, abroad and at work.

And tomorrow was God's Theophany.

A New Heart
and a New Spirit

O come, let us worship and fall down before Him,
and let us weep before the Lord Who made us.
For He is our God, and we are the people of His
pasture and the sheep of His hand.

(Psalm 94:6-7)

He could feel the rhythm of the waves under Stavros's fishing boat, as it bobbed in the brilliant Mediterranean waters.

"You take the net, George; lower it and see how you do."

"Are we far enough from the shore?"

"Yes."

He dreamt next of the beauty of the sunrise that morning as they had turned the energetically bouncing boat back towards its dock.

But when George opened his eyes, it was to find himself squeezed into a 747 beside his wife Maria. The airplane, like Stavros's boat, moved back and forth in turbulence.

"So you're awake," said Maria, lifting a cup of Coca-Cola to her lips. "Did you sleep well? You missed most of the movie."

"I was dreaming of the island," he said.

"I don't understand why you liked it so much; such a small house, and those boys of theirs run wild. Panagiota says she has to wash the salt-water off their clothes almost every day. Just think if Demetri had grown up like that."

George frowned and said nothing. He thought of the last time he had visited their son. Hunched on a metal chair, he had talked very little to his father sitting on the other side of the glass partition. The words that continually rang in George's ears were: "You failed me, Dad. How could you let me end up in here?"

Demetri's own deeds had landed him in the prison; George knew

54

that, but all the same it hurt him deeply to hear his son blame him. Perhaps it was his fault; perhaps he had been too indulgent a parent.

He knew that Maria blamed no one; rather, loving the sinner and hating the sin, she stood firm as always. But George had become so dismayed that he began questioning the Faith as he had done years ago on the threshold of adulthood, trying to understand if the beliefs his parents had handed down to him were true and right or not.

Maria laid her hand comfortingly over his on the narrow arm-rest, as if reading his thoughts. "Don't worry about it," she said. "Just pray for him; God will help him to realize his mistakes some day."

"If it isn't too late by then."

"Where's your trust in Christ, George?"

He didn't answer.

"Well, without it, you're in no shape to judge even our son."

"He's sinned; anyone can see that!"

"But God forgives, and we must forgive as well."

"Demetri doesn't want forgiveness."

"He's human; he must want love. To show him we care is the least we can do."

"Oh, that should do a lot of good. The boy goes off and deserts us, then blames us for his mistakes, and that makes you think he wants love from us? He had all the love a child could want, but what good did it do? It only gave him a big ego and a disregard for anyone but himself."

Maria tightened her grasp on his hand and shook his whole arm. "You stop this, George. Sit and pray until you're ready to think like a Christian. I don't want to have to listen to you talk this way."

He frowned at his wife and turned his head away, missing the sea and the little boat and the freedom from every care and responsibility that he and Stavros had enjoyed, fishing because they wanted to, not because they had to.

The next day in his studio, George took out a large piece of canvas and pinned it taut against a wooden frame. He arranged his brushes and chose his pre-mixed paints, then sat on the drawing stool a long time with his eyes closed. After a while the picture came vividly to him: first a sky that would take one's breath away on three quarters of the canvas, all the lovely sunrise colors blazing out together—pink and orange, yellow, red, blue, and purple—and below it a sea with large white-capped waves and a small boat moving to the sweet motion of the water where it rested. There would also be two birds flying above the sea and a thin strip of land off to the left just beginning to glow with the morning light.

He made several thumbnail sketches on a piece of paper, but, being impatient, decided to forgo a pencil drawing on the canvas and start painting immediately.

George had taken his brush in hand and begun the first few strokes of sunrise when something caused him to look up at Photios Kontoglou's tender icon of St. Symeon the God-Receiver hanging on the wall. The brush almost fell from his fingers. What were those eyes of the saint commanding him? George laid the brush, still wet with paint, across the water jar, scooted back in his seat, and pulled out one of the drawers under his art desk. The top item, something he had put aside weeks or months ago, was an unfinished sketch of the same icon of St. Symeon. That loving, compunctionate look in his face as he gazed at the Christ Child in his arms was full of the Holy Spirit. How long it was since George had regarded his Lord with any similar feeling!

Overcome with guilt more than anything else, he hurriedly put back the picture and shoved the drawer closed, rolled the stool towards his canvas again and resumed his painting. Yet in his heart he felt troubled. An artist to his finger-tips and an iconographer by career, lately George had been neglecting his holy work and doing only secular kinds of art. Today St. Symeon himself seemed to be crying out to him to go back to painting icons, but to no avail. George refused to listen; he was happy with his picture of the Greek island.

Yet the paint spattered more than it should, and somehow he had ended up with too much red in the sky. That had to be counteracted with a little pink and yellow. Then the yellow he had chosen turned out to be too bright, and it swallowed up the expansive space. He spilled the blue paint; after which he knocked over the water jar. It ran into his pallet and ruined the paints arranged there.

All in all, by lunchtime George had accomplished very little. Maria was at work, so he made himself a sandwich and ate it as he worked. An unwise move, however. A sticky glob of strawberry jelly dripped out onto the handle of his paintbrush, and somehow he managed to get both jelly and peanut-butter on the canvas itself.

George glanced up at St. Symeon again. His guilt increased. Shuffling through his papers after lunch, he found many orders of icons yet to be filled. The oldest of them was from his parish priest, a gentle man named Father Leontius. He had requested that copy of Photios Kontoglou's St. Symeon the God-Receiver. Father hadn't even reminded George about it; not that he had forgotten, but that he was too kind to mention it.

George was drawn away from these thoughts by the sound of the side door opening and very shortly after that a few scales being played on the viola. Elpitha, their niece, often came over after school.

He seated himself on the stool again and began painting, this time concentrating on the first undercoat of the sea.

He had just finished sketching around where the land was supposed to be when Elpitha knocked on the door of the studio.

"Come in!" called George.

"What are you working on now?"

He showed her the canvas, describing as best he could how he hoped the finished picture would appear.

"No icons?" She sounded disappointed.

George shook his head.

"I brought my sketches to show you. Do you want to see them?"

"All right." He dipped his brush in the water jar and laid it on his paper towel, swiveling around on the stool to face her.

She was flipping through the pages of her sketchbook until she reached a drawing she had made of Christ.

"I used a grid like you told me," said Elpitha. "This is by Photios Kontoglou."

"Yes, it looks like his work. Are you going to ink it in?"

She nodded. "I already did my second one in ink." She turned the page; it was a beautiful copy of Kontoglou's "Directress" icon.

"How long did this take you?" asked George, impressed.

"Not too long. Maybe two days."

Her evident enthusiasm was contagious. "Two days? Wow! You have a gift from God."

"Well, I was so excited about it that I did it right away, you know."

"Have you done any more?"

"Not yet."

"Can I see them again?"

She gave him her sketchbook.

"These are good. You should keep drawing."

She smiled a little shyly. "I'm glad you like them."'

"Yes, they're really nice."

"Thanks."

He handed them back at last.

"I just came by to show them to you," said Elpitha. "Now I have to get home."

"How's the viola going?"

"Fine. We have a concert in two weeks. But I have to go. See you later, Uncle George."

"Bye, Elpitha."

She waved before shutting the studio door behind her and leaving him once more in peace. Peace as in "quiet;" not peace as in "peace of mind."

He got up and went to see if the mail had come yet. It was a good excuse to leave behind his guilt over the neglect of his icon orders.

Bills and ads, catalogs—a letter from Demetri jumped out at him. The prison stamp glared. George set down the rest of the mail and tore open the envelope.

Dear Mom and Dad,
How are you guys?
Don't forget I'll be free and home in ten days. I'm going to need
some money fast. Also, could you look around for a really cheap apart-
ment for me? And I'll need some job ads. Anything in the construc-
tion field would be good.
Have you seen Julia lately? Half the time when I call, she isn't there.
Thanks, Mom, for the food you sent. I hope you two have gotten
over this theft thing by now. It really wasn't a big deal. The truth is,
I only stole two TVs and a stereo. I wasn't involved in the rest. And
those drugs they found belonged to Terry. I swear I never got hooked
on them. You've got to believe me about that.
See you in ten days. I'm coming on the 6:30 bus. Don't forget to be
there with Julia.

Demetri

George read the letter through twice. Amazingly enough Demetri sounded more affectionate towards them than usual. But he didn't sound very repentant, and George was sorry to learn that he hadn't forgotten about his punk girlfriend Julia.

Maria opened the front door and entered the hall.

"Hello, dear. Is that a letter?"

"Yes. It's from Demetri."

"Really?"

He handed her the page, and she read it quickly.

"Well? What do you think of it?" said George.

"He needs our love, George. He really does."

"Maybe."

"There's no 'maybe' about it. He does need us—more than ever now." She took off her purse and put it down.

"Oh, he'll never change," said George. "He's not sorry for what he did. We've waited years for him to change. You said when he graduated from college he would start to see things more clearly, but he dropped out and never did graduate. Then you said once he fell in love he'd have to change. Instead, he chooses a girl with fewer morals than he has himself. I'm tired of waiting for something to happen; nothing's doing him any good."

"George, George, we have to have patience. If God isn't hearing our prayers, there must be something wrong with how we're praying.

Don't you see? There's nothing we can do but pray for him. He has to change himself; he's his own man now, not just our dear little son."

George didn't answer.

"How's your work coming?" asked Maria, to change the subject.

"Fine." He hadn't told her that it was several weeks now since he had touched iconography. He thought of the painting of the Greek island sitting on his drawing table. It wasn't very good art; he had better throw it out rather than finish it. Nothing was worth doing anyway, as long as he was sunk in this depression. His life was meaningless; God had abandoned them all. Maria's optimism must only be a mask to hide her own despair. So he thought.

After dinner, Maria went to the store and George to his studio again. Outside, the light dimmed; he closed the curtains over his tall studio windows and turned on the bright lights to make a false daylight. Then he mounted his stool and looked at the half-painted canvas before him.

He sat motionless for half an hour or more, simply gazing at the picture. He was back on the island, he was stepping into the boat and sailing away from everything but the sky and the brilliant blue water.

He swung around on the stool to find a color he had forgotten to take out, and there lay a small piece of paper with a sketch of an icon on it. It must have slid out of Elpitha's sketchbook. George picked it up and examined it closely. It was St. George—his own patron saint— one of the first icons he had ever tried when he was learning iconography. Every small detail was perfect, the shading delicate and beautiful—the face and hair, the armor and the cape, all simply and excellently drawn and outlined with pen and ink.

Elpitha must have spent a long time on this; only a dedicated person would attempt an icon so small. George took out his ruler and measured it: scarcely one-and-a-half inches square! As he continued to look closely at the icon, he felt a thrill of the old joy he had experienced when he had first started learning iconography. Every new face had held a challenge for him. Could he draw the lines correctly and trace over each shadow until it reached its appropriate darkness? Could he blend the colors smoothly, could he paint each hair-thin mark exactly as it was meant to be? With God's help, yes! With the skill and talent God had vouchsafed him, yes!

Setting down Elpitha's icon of St. George, he turned back to his drawing table and with a sudden motion grabbed the messy canvas and threw it into the trash. He opened the drawer and pulled out his sketch of St. Symeon the God-Receiver. Laying it on the slanted table, he searched for a properly sharp pencil.

The fire had entered him; he was full of enthusiasm; he would make this icon so that all people could kiss and revere the likeness of holy St. Symeon, who once held Christ the Saviour in his very arms!

George had picked up his pencil, but stopped in mid-air and put it down again. He stood up, facing the icons, and prayed as he hadn't prayed in a long time that God would grant him mercy and help him in his work.

Afterwards, he sat down once more and finished the drawing of St. Symeon with no trouble.

The ten days leading up to Demetri's return soon dwindled into two, one, and finally it was the actual day itself. Neither George nor Maria had spoken to Julia about meeting him at the bus station, but maybe she already knew when he was to come. They had almost certainly corresponded while he was in prison.

"Are you ready yet?" George spoke irritably because he was worried. How would he speak to his son? He hadn't seen him in such a long time. How could they ever manage to carry on a normal conversation?

Maria hurried downstairs. "I'm ready." She grabbed her purse. "Let's go. We don't want to keep him waiting."

They got into the car.

"Did you look for an apartment like he asked you to, George?"

"There's some place that's not too expensive on Lamont Avenue."

"Is that a safe neighborhood?"

He shrugged.

"How about a job for him?"

"I saved the Classified section of the Sunday paper."

There was nothing more to say until they reached the station. George could sense that Maria too was a little nervous about this meeting with their son, for there was a marked difference between Demetri the juvenile delinquent and Demetri the ex-convict.

By the time they arrived, parked, and got out of the car, a small group of people had gathered to wait for the bus. It had been due ten minutes ago, they said, but it hadn't yet made an appearance.

George and Maria joined the others, seating themselves on a bench. They waited and waited. Gradually some of the people began drifting away, grumbling about buses and bus drivers. It started to rain—just sprinkles at first, followed by a heavy downpour.

Maria looked worriedly at her husband. "Where do you think he is?"

"I don't know."

Their hair was dripping with rain, and they got up and moved into a covered bus-stop.

Soon Maria said, "What do you think we should do?"

"Well, I hate to say we should go home."

"Is there a way to call and see if the bus ever left its first station?"

"Yes, but it could be stalled for some reason at any one of the stops along the way."

"I guess you're right."

George looked at his watch. "It's been over an hour," he said.

"I don't want to leave because what if he comes really late and no one's here to greet him? Where could that bus be?" said Maria, following the road with her eyes.

"Yes, but maybe we should go home. He can call us if he gets here later tonight."

"I don't want to, but I suppose you're right."

They both got up and stepped out into the pouring rain towards their car.

The moment they were over the threshold of the house, the phone rang.

George went into the kitchen and picked up the receiver.

"Mr. Papadopoulos?"

"Yes?"

"We've been trying to reach you; your son Demetrios has been in a car accident."

"What?! Who is this? What happened?"

"This is Dr. Lang at St. Catherine's Hospital."

"But—what happened?"

"The bus your son was on was hit by a car and turned on its side. Demetrios has a minor concussion, a broken arm, and a sprained ankle. It's not too serious—he should be much better in a few days."

"Can we come and see him right away?"

"Yes, of course."

"All right. Thank you, Doctor."

"Goodbye."

George put the phone back on the hook and turned to face the frightened eyes of Maria.

"What's happened?" she said. "It's Demetri, isn't it?"

He nodded.

"That was a doctor. Is he all right?" she said.

"Get your umbrella. I'll tell you in the car."

Demetri lay in the hospital bed, unaware of what was happening around him. He saw in his cloudy memory a car coming out of nowhere, smashing into the bus and tipping it before skidding back across the road. As if in slow motion, the bus had fallen onto its side in the grass beside the street. Demetri, flung from his seat, twisted his ankle around the seat leg and cracked his arm as he fell on top of someone else. And then smoke and sirens, and he opened his eyes to find himself here—in this white place. Where was "here?" He had no idea.

He gazed at his arm; it too was white. He tried moving it away from his stomach, but it seemed to be attached to him by some sort of ribbon. His head ached, and his eyes refused to focus. But whenever he closed them he saw the accident re-enacted in his feverish brain, over and over again.

At the other end of the room a woman dressed in white was doing something. Perhaps his mother? How long it seemed since he had seen his mother. And his father, too. Something had prevented him from seeing them, he knew, but it was difficult to think what.

"Oh, you're awake." Coming over to his side, the woman smiled at him.

Demetri saw that she was not his mother, but a thin girl with light brown hair. "Who are you?" he asked.

"I'm Nadya." She still smiled.

"Can you tell me why I'm here?"

"So we can take care of you. Look, you're hurt." She pointed to his bandaged arm in its sling.

"Oh. I guess I am."

She gave him a cup of liquid. "Drink this for the pain."

"But I don't feel any pain."

"You're still in shock," she said. "How is your head?"

"It feels weird."

"Yes? Would it help to have a cool, wet cloth on your forehead?"

"I don't know."

"I'll get one." She went over to the tiny bathroom and ran cold water over a white towel.

"Do you know my name?" he asked, feeling strange and a little giddy.

"Demetrios Papadopoulos."

"Yes; Demetrios Papadopoulos. Isn't that a funny name?" He laughed. "And who are you again?"

"Nadya—it's short for Nadezhda."

"That's funny too."

"I'm from Russia," said Nadya. "My sister and I came here four years ago."

The door opened and Dr. Lang entered, talking over his shoulder to

George and Maria.

"Demetri!" Maria rushed to her son's bedside and knelt beside him. "Oh, Demetri, Demetri!" She laughed and cried at once.

"Mom? Is it really you?"

"Yes, darling, it's me!"

George stood behind her, looking unsure of what to say.

Demetri saw him and grinned, feeling bewildered. "Dad? Mom and Dad? I haven't seen you two in a long time!"

"We know, son, we know."

"I feel so confused. I don't know—whatever it was that happened to me—I'm just all shaken up."

"It's all right," said Maria. "Calm down. You don't have to talk about it now. We're just so happy that you're okay."

"We were worried about you," said George.

"Dad," said Demetri, "I—where have you two been all this time?"

"Waiting for you, darling," Maria told him, holding his hand between her own.

George nodded. "You were just coming home—remember?"

Demetri yawned. "Home . . ." he said, in a dazed voice.

"Maybe you should get some rest," said Maria. "We'll come again tomorrow and see how you're feeling, Demetri."

"Yes, yes, come again." He lay back against the pillow and put a hand to his head.

Dr. Lang escorted George and Maria out of the room.

"How's your head?" asked Nadya.

But he was already asleep.

In dreams, Demetri wandered through empty prison corridors and fell endlessly in buses that were overturned. Once or twice he was conscious for a few seconds of Nadya, bending over him to put a fresh towel on his forehead or sitting beside him in case he should wake up and want something.

Perhaps two or three hours past midnight Demetri felt a hand touch him, and he was instantly alert in all his senses. By his bed, with one hand on his wounded arm and the other holding a golden box, stood a young man with curly hair. His face, when Demetri gazed up at it, was radiant with light; and all around him hung a beautiful fragrance. He looked so familiar, but Demetri couldn't think who he was or where he had seen him before.

The man opened the box he carried and dipped a small spoon into it. Then he put the spoon to Demetri's lips, and Demetri swallowed the liquid given him. For a moment, he didn't know if he dreamt or was awake. His soul was flooded with such joy, such peaceful joy, unlike any feeling he had ever known! And then all at once his head felt clear, and he knew who he was and where he was and why.

"St. Panteleimon!" he cried, just as the saint departed from him.

Peace flowing through him, Demetri fell back asleep.

When he awoke in the morning, his mind still felt clear. Remembering the bus accident and how close he had come to death the day before, the way his thoughts had clogged together, and finally the wondrous healing vision, he decided to try praying. It was something Demetri hadn't done in years, but he felt that some thanks were due to the Saviour Who had kept him from death and even sent St. Panteleimon the Healer to his bedside.

God did exist—he had always felt it inside, even during the worst times of his life. Throughout the sloth, the delinquency, and the breaking of his parents' hearts, Demetri had always known that what he did was wrong, and that God saw it all. But he had also felt that he was too far gone ever to turn back and fall down before the Lord's feet. And there was no need to worry yet, he had thought, because he was young and healthy. Repentance and death and eternity—those things were for old people on their deathbeds.

Yet now he saw that death could indeed come to anyone at any moment. *I could've been killed*, he told himself again and again, *but God decided to save me.*

Nadya came in to see if he wanted anything.

"Some water, please," said Demetri.

She got it for him.

"You said you're from Russia, right?" he asked her.

"Yes, I've only been in this country for four years."

"Then—are you Orthodox?"

Nadya looked surprised. "Yes, actually, I am."

"I used to be Orthodox too," Demetri said. "I used to go to church with my parents." He paused. "But I'm a horrible person—a criminal. I... God could have taken my life yesterday. I don't know why He didn't." He drank the water she had brought him and handed back the cup. "Do you believe in miracles?" he asked her. "You know— visions of saints and things like that."

Nadya nodded. "Yes, I think so."

"My mind was so confused," he said, "but now I can see every- thing—all my sins, crimes... It must have been hard for my parents..."

"Don't worry," said Nadya. "Anyone can see that they love you very much."

"I should've realized," Demetri said. "I did realize, but I guess I didn't care. I wish I had. I should have thought about them before..."

"I'm sure it's not too late."

"Do you think God saved my life for a reason?"

"It's possible. I don't know."

"Anyway, He's giving me another chance, isn't He?"

"Yes," said Nadya, "He is."

"Do you think we should tell Julia?" said George.

"No." Maria shook her head. "She isn't a good influence on him. Besides, maybe this bump on his head has made him forget all about her."

"Isn't that being a little too optimistic?"

"Maybe."

The door-bell rang, and George went to open the door.

On the front step stood Julia herself, holding a smoking cigarette between her fingers, her eyes glittering and hair dyed black—possi- bly to match the black, silver-studded clothes she wore.

"Is Demetri here?" she said, peering into the hall. "I couldn't make it last night."

"No, he isn't here," said Maria, over George's shoulder.

"Where is he?"

Neither of them said anything.

"Where is he?" she said again, this time with a note of irritation.

"He's in the hospital."

"Are you serious? What happened?"

"It was a car accident."

"Really? Is he okay?"

"He's all right," said George. "It could have been a lot worse."

"'Well, are you going to see him?"

"We—"

"I'm sure you won't mind if I come along. I'll just follow you in my car." She ran her fingers through her unnaturally black hair, tossing her cigarette onto the front step and crushing it with her heel.

George and Maria exchanged glances.

"What are we going to do now?" said Maria, as Julia walked down the yard to her car.

"We don't have much choice," George told her. "Just say your prayers."

They locked the front door, got in the car, and slid out of the driveway, watching Julia start up her engine and zoom in close behind them.

Nadya left the room when they arrived. Demetri looked up and smiled, happy to see both his parents. Then his eyes fell on the other figure with them. Julia—that black-haired rebel, so cool and careless… how easy to join her and the others again, to slip back into that rut, to hurt his parents again… But God had saved him; God had sent him St. Panteleimon the Healer; God cared.

She smiled. "What's going on, Demetri?" she said. "How do you feel?"

"I'm okay."

"Is your head any better, dear?" asked Maria.

"Yeah, it feels clearer."

"Sorry I couldn't get here yesterday," said Julia, ignoring Demetri's parents.

"It's all right, Julia. What I want to know is where you were all those times I called and no one answered the phone."

"I was out—no big deal."

He didn't say anything.

"You weren't jealous, were you?" She stepped closer.

"Why—should I have been?"

She shrugged. "Just hoped you were over that whole possessive stage," she said.

"You cheated on me, didn't you? I know you did—while I was out of the way in jail."

"Demetri, I'm not your property, you know."

"Wouldn't want you to be," he said.

"Oh? I wouldn't have thought that from your letters."

Demetri looked into her face; there was nothing wrong with it in terms of physical beauty, but something ugly stared out through her eyes.

"Why are you looking at me like that?" she said, frowning.

"Julia, just get out of my face."

"What's wrong with you, Demetri?"

"Nothing. But things aren't the same between us anymore."

"Well, that's obvious."

"So, whatever I said in my letters, that was then—I'm not the same person anymore."

"Oh, you're not?" She was mocking now. "Are you a changed man, Demetri? Should I call a priest?"

"Julia—" He reined in the curses at his lips. "Just leave me alone! Go back to your pitiful little friends and live your pitiful life with them. You know they don't really care about anyone but themselves, and I don't think you do either."

"So you suddenly care about everyone?" she said.

"You know what?" Demetri told her. "I could've died yesterday, but God decided to let me live. You'd better pray that He gives you a second chance, because I doubt that you'll ever change on your own."

She laughed. "Great—he's a preacher now. You must be so proud," she said, turning to his parents, who had stood silently watching this scene.

Demetri groaned.

"Well, hope your head gets a little clearer," she said. "Don't be a fool. You know there's no God. And if there were, He wouldn't care if you lived or died." And Julia left the room.

The confrontation had distressed Demetri.

"Where is Nadya?" he said.

"I—I don't know." Maria and George came forward.

"Demetri, I didn't know you even believed in God anymore," said George.

"Dad, I do—I do!"

He looked at his mother; her eyes shone with tears. "You really aren't going to go back to your old friends?" she said.

Demetri shook his head. "They aren't my friends. They aren't anybody's friends—just a group of people who are desperate to hide from God. And I don't want to have to hide from Him anymore."

When at last Demetri returned home—to the home of his youth—he saw everything with new eyes. Beauty and grace were all around him; good things he had never noticed before put the old evil to death with their brilliance.

George happily showed him into the studio again. There on his drawing table, dry and complete, lay a beautiful icon of St. Symeon the God-Receiver.

The Brighter the Stars

Say not that salvation has ceased to exist,
That sorrows have trampled upon you roughshod:
The darker the night is, the brighter the stars,
The deeper the suffering, the closer is God . . .

A. N. Maikov

Leaning elbow and hip against the crumbling balcony, ignoring a siren that wailed through the streets below, Mahmoud Caspari peered through his telescope and jotted notes in Farsi.

"First appeared two weeks ago. Star gone supernova? Maybe millions of years ago, light just arriving . . ."

"Mahmoud! Time to pray."

"Coming." He blinked, and his eyes watered with strain from the telescope. Prayer again. He fulfilled his required prayers religiously, but not fanatically. Tonight, if he had his way, he would have asked for more time, so he could document the star, for whatever good it would do him now. Once he would have wanted to write about it, maybe even produce *the* article that would make Mahmoud Caspari a household name—or at least a classroom name—in the field of astronomy. Now it didn't matter, and besides, God called. With a last glance at the great star shining down from the heavens, he snapped his notebook shut and went inside.

Here in Iran he felt something in the air, a tension, a sense that Allah was close. America lacked it. In Iran a Muslim could believe in *jihad*, warfare for Allah; you could almost feel it flowing through your body as you walked through the streets. It was louder than America, hotter, dustier, somehow harsher.

It wasn't comforting.

In the close mustiness of the house, Mahmoud blinked again, pulling his glasses off to pat at his eyes. They didn't hurt, but he never touched them except gingerly. Touching them tore open festering wounds in his soul, and deep inside him he felt the turmoil boiling up again, rushing into his throat to pour out in Persian screams, but he swallowed them down. He was home. True, he had return tickets to

New York and was expected to teach three classes in the spring semester, but for now he was in Iran. He was home.

"There is no god but Allah, and Muhammad is his prophet."

Every Muslim knew things happened that were beyond man's control. Men lived with them. But if it had been anything but his eyes! A man's eyes were his life, the light of his body, and what good were they covered with scales? He was young for cataracts, but they were growing over his eyes, and even if the doctors operated, he might never regain his former sight. Probably he never would. With his sight clouded, he wasn't much of an astronomer, and his hopes of tenure died like an imploding galaxy. The years in America, the years of English, the degrees, the publications were dust in the solar wind. The eyes didn't hurt. But they saw less and less. Although for now he could still read, and could still use his telescope, he knew it wouldn't last.

"There is no god but Allah—"

For the first time in his life, Mahmoud doubted. What if there was no God at all? Certainly there was no God for a son of Islam who had abandoned Iran and gone to live in America. Such a person was no better than dirt, no better than a Westerner. He was half a man with less than half his eyes, and Allah was not a merciful god.

There were no merciful gods. Because if there had been, they would have left Mahmoud his dreams.

Early the next morning, pouring over astronomy journals he had brought with him, he discovered a brief note: "A star, presumed supernova, was first noticed on December 1 at 9:45 p.m. by an Israeli astronomer based in Bethlehem." As it went on to describe the astronomer and the star, Mahmoud bit down on his disappointment. Then the star he had been taking notes on last night wasn't anything new. December 1, the note said. Of course. For word of it to have appeared in this journal, it would have to have been sighted before Mahmoud even left home. No sense in what he was doing, then. No sense in straining his eyes. Not his name but that of an Israeli would figure in the articles that would appear about his star. Instead of continuing to study it, he should forget about it and savor his remaining time in Iran.

Pulling off his thick glasses, he massaged his eyes, resolving to put his telescope away in his suitcase where it belonged. It was time for prayer again, or soon it would be. Pushing his glasses back on, Mahmoud went to pray in formulas that slid off his tongue like oil, while his heart stirred within him and whispered that there was no Allah.

The star oppressed him. Hanging night after night in the sky, it lit his room while he tossed in the Iranian winter cool. It seemed to shine into his heart, which was a cold thing now, full of dead ashes: his burning hopes, the fire of Islam. All dead. There was no God. He mouthed prayers by rote, hating them, hating himself and his uselessness. When he went back to America, he would teach the spring semester, and then what? Oh, he could use what time remained to him to try to advance in his chosen field, but they were prejudiced against him already, his fellow professors who resented an Iranian who could match their knowledge. On some level he didn't care what they thought.

On some level he wanted to cry.

Fate was to be accepted. Mahmoud knew it. But there was the star, mocking him. He despised it. If he had still hoped for tenure, he would have rerouted his return trip through Tel Aviv and taken a day or two in Bethlehem to speak to the Israeli astronomer who had seen the star before him. He could still do that, but he wouldn't, he wouldn't, his hopes were dead, the astronomer was a worthless Jew, and Mahmoud was a wretch who would soon be blind. What point was there in going now? To try to salvage his career? His career had vanished in a doctor's office. Why should he care if the star seemed to peer in at him like a live thing? It was only gases and fires, like the fire of faith that he lacked. He wouldn't go to Bethlehem. He wouldn't. Why should he want to?

Who knew? God knew. If he went, Mahmoud would be doing something besides pitying himself.

He was a fool.

Israel. Bethlehem in the evening on January 6, and after a long ride on a sputtering bus, Mahmoud haggled with an Israeli hotel owner who eyed him askance, probably taking him, a Persian from Iran, for an Arab, as had the two before this man who claimed they had no empty rooms. If he'd known Bethlehem better, maybe he could have found his way to the Arab quarter, where they were at least all Muslims, but as an exhausted first-time visitor he would settle for what he could find.

All the same, as he emerged onto the street after a meal, he breathed out with released tension, for half-blind or not he hadn't missed the glances towards him over shoulders while he ate, or the low-voiced conversations in English that switched to Hebrew as he passed.

With the setting January sun, the star shone out more brightly than in Iran, spreading white light in Mahmoud's path, like a carpet leading down to the Christian hell of torments he had learned about in history. *What need have I to go there?* Mahmoud thought. *I who live in torments.* But he lifted his face to the sky, although the few other people on the streets hurried along with their heads down.

A magnificent star, magnificent, even half-blurred; it almost made Mahmoud, despite his misery, want to set pen to paper in a flowing Persian poem. It distracted him from himself.

Odd how it seemed to hover over Bethlehem. True, a Middle Eastern sky could feel close enough to reach up to and lay your palm against, while American skies floated far overhead, but he would swear that between his leaving Iran and his arrival in Bethlehem, the star had dropped nearer and had *grown*. Had the Israeli astronomer noticed as much? Perhaps Mahmoud should document it, but for that he would need the notebook in his suitcase.

Hurrying back to his hotel in the starlit night, he caught his toe in the uneven pavement and flew forward, losing his glasses and the skin of his palms in the jar of landing, and hissed an American curse, and offered no prayer afterwards for forgiveness. God who was taking his sight, what did He care for Mahmoud? The god of Muhammad cared for those who lashed the infidel, not those who struggled to wrest their living from a foreign country.

Where were his glasses? He needed to see, to what extent he still could, and he blinked in starlight, dazzled by it . . . and shuddered all at once, as if he were no longer utterly alone; as if a Presence that he couldn't identify had drawn near to him.

Was he still alone? He was. Wasn't he? He must see.

"Mahmoud Caspari! Why do you not believe in me?"

His name. Here, in the streets of Bethlehem, and in such a Voice, resounding in his head; blinking his worthless eyes, Mahmoud scrabbled behind him for his glasses, but his fingers touched only pavement, and he saw nothing of Whoever had approached him. Gasping, he worked to unclamp his tongue from the roof of his mouth. "Who are you, sir?"

In what language had the Voice spoken? In English or Farsi or Arabic or in some other, unknown tongue which Mahmoud had somehow understood? In what language had Mahmoud answered?

"I am One in Whom you do not believe."

Allah? No. If Allah spoke, it would be like thunder and lightening, but this, though full of power, was quieter, gentler, like a breeze touching Mahmoud's heart with loving hands. This was what Mahmoud wanted from God, but it wasn't what he had once believed in and now doubted. Swallowing hard, he repeated, "Who are You, Lord?"

"I am Jesus, the Son of God, in Whom you do not believe."

The Voice resonated with authority, but not with cruelty. Cruelty from such a Voice would be impossible; but oh, there might be stern mercy. But for a reason. And yet . . . Surely Mahmoud dreamed all of this, and would wake from it in the morning. "I believe in You as a prophet."

"I am not a prophet but the Son of the Living God. Now rise and return to your hotel, and tomorrow go early to the church of My Nativity, and there you will learn what you must do."

In the deserted street, the star's light shone brighter and brighter, until Mahmoud clasped his hands over his eyes, while voices sweeter than hearing praised the Christian God, but Mahmoud stumbled to his feet and fled from them, noticing one thing only as he ran: the crunch of glass and a plastic frame beneath his feet.

Tossing in bed, he heard the Voice in his dreams whenever he slept, saying, "I am Jesus, the Son of God, in Whom you do not believe," but towards morning Mahmoud roused with another whisper running through his thoughts: *"It is time."*

Time for what? Time to go to the Church of the Nativity? But he was blind with his glasses broken, to say nothing of the cataracts. And he was a Muslim. Yet the Voice drew him, promising a God of love, and he thought that with such a God even blindness would be bearable.

Since he was awake, he could do worse than get up; dressed, he decided, blind or not, to go out into the city for a breath of air—no, who was he fooling? Although he didn't know where the Church of the Nativity was, he was hoping to find it somehow. His feet led him... he didn't know where, and what should have been landmarks swam past him in a blur of beige, but he found his way at last through a door into crowded darkness.

Surely he had left sanity somewhere in Iran. Surely God took no interest in him, as he had decided lately, and who had ever heard of God accosting a man as he walked down the street and calling him to follow Him? Oh, the Christians had some similar story, but—

I am Jesus, the Son of God, in Whom you do not believe.

But he, Mahmoud, was a Muslim.

What place did he stand in now, that he could hear chanting? All around him he heard and felt a press of people, pushing him forward, and extending his hand, he reached out with his fingertips, sparing his poor lacerated palm, until he brushed the rough coolness of a wall. At one with the crowd, he began to make his blind way further into the building, stumbling a little down a flight of steps, hearing the chanting receding in the distance, still audible, but fainter.

The Cave of the Nativity

I am Jesus, the Son of God, in Whom you do not believe.

The further Mahmoud penetrated into the dark building, the more the distant chanting reached into his soul, losing him in unfamiliar languages mixed with Arabic. "Lord, have mercy," the choir chanted in Arabic. "Lord, have mercy." Mercy. As another phrase jumped out at him: "Father, Son, and Holy Spirit, One God," Mahmoud realized with a hammering of his heart that he had entered a Christian church, maybe even the Church of the Nativity where the Voice had told him to go. If so, where were the instructions the Voice had promised him? Here he would learn what he must do . . .

No, he didn't want to learn. He wanted to go on being a Muslim, and forget that the God of the Christians had concerned Himself with him . . . but on the thought he began to tremble, for the Voice he had heard last night had resonated with power and grace; how dare he turn his back on such a God? Besides, a God who had cared to concern Himself was no God to disdain.

Somewhere beyond Mahmoud, the Christian choir went on asking for mercy.

Mercy. Mercy. It was all Mahmoud had wanted, all that had brought him out into the city this morning and into this church where God had surely led him. Would the God Christ have mercy on Mahmoud the blind? If he ought to cry out to his own god, to Muhammad's Allah, where were the words? Allah had no mercy, he knew that. Shaking, clenching his scraped hands tight against the cool of the wall, he raised his eyes to a bright blur of candles near him. Mercy. It trembled on his tongue. "Have mercy." There, he had spoken to the Christian God, asking Him for mercy, and he held his breath for thunder from heaven, sent from Muhammad's god, to strike him down.

Instead the choir, in a thunder of praise: "Christ is born; give ye glory! Christ is come from heaven; receive ye Him! Christ is on earth; be ye exalted!"

Letting out his breath measure by measure, Mahmoud tried a new phrase on his tongue: "Father, Son, and Holy Spirit."

Blasphemy. What was he, a Muslim, doing saying such things? What was he doing here at all? In a Christian church in Bethlehem, having been spoken to by the Christian God...But it didn't matter. Christ offered mercy, or so His followers believed. Allah was implacable. There was a word for men who did what Mahmoud was thinking: apostate.

The Place where Christ was born

On some level he didn't care. With his clouded eyes still fixed on the candles, he opened his heart, admitted the grace of this church and the hope of mercy into his soul. "Lord Jesus Christ, Son of God, in Whom I might come to believe, help me!"

As he cried out to the Christian God, the floodgates of his tears opened, pouring down his cheeks from his blind eyes to scour him clean, until he felt empty and refreshed, and blinking the stinging salt from his eyes, he focused on the candles... but instead of candles, he saw that they were a ring of oil lamps around a silver star in the floor.

He saw them. Without glasses, as clear as if the cataracts had never existed, he saw them, and beyond them he saw the crowd parting for a Christian priest in a cassock, whom maybe Mahmoud could stop and speak to, to ask him whether this was the place where the Virgin the Christians told about had borne the Christ Child, and maybe the priest would go on from there and explain the Christian faith.

Leaning against the firm rail of his apartment's balcony, Boulus *
Caspari peered through his telescope and jotted notes in Farsi. As he
bent forward, adjusting the telescope, against his chest through the
open neck of his shirt gleamed a gold cross…

Six months ago, in Bethlehem, he had stood outside the Church of
the Nativity and watched the great star that he had seen hover over it,
as it or another like it had hovered over the cave where the Christ
Child was born. A day later the star disappeared, if it had ever been
anywhere but in Boulus' noetic sight, and although he scanned every
word of his astronomy journal, he found no mention of any new stars,
presumed supernova or otherwise.

Today, as he studied the heavens, he murmured under his breath
over and over, "Lord Jesus Christ, Son of God, in Whom I believe,
have mercy on me, a sinner."

Now his family shunned him, and Iran was closed to him. It didn't
matter. The true God had stripped the physical scales and the scales
of unbelief from his eyes. God—the God of love—had shown mercy.

---

* Arabic form of Paul.

God's Fire

Fr. George stood in church before the icon of Christ's Nativity, praying. He didn't pray audibly, but fervently in his heart asked God to teach his parishioners to remember His Birth in a holy and good way. The gift-giving, the carols, the merriment and feasting were empty without thoughts of the true celebration at hand. He, too, felt empty today – Christmas Eve and no words to tell his spiritual children how to care about the feast, no words to preach gently and touch their hearts. There must be some new way that he could explain to them the glory of the Birth of Christ. He prayed, lowering his head, asking in humility for the Saviour's help.

Outside, an orange sky illumined the beautiful church with its glow. Less than an hour now until the Christmas Eve service. Non-Orthodox pedestrians, who had forgotten their holiday thirteen days ago, shuffled or hurried past the building, lost in their own musings. A slight wind stirred the black points of leafless trees silhouetted against the sunset. At first no one noticed that the wintry smell of smoke from house chimneys grew stronger around the church; no one saw the growing gray cloud or the bright flames rising up fiercely to meet the reddish sky.

Inside, Fr. George remained lost in his prayer, completely unaware of any danger.

A girl walking by with her mother stopped and sniffed the air. She tugged at her mother's coat-sleeve. "Mom, it smells like fire."

"It's someone's fireplace."

"Are you sure?"

The girl sniffed harder, glancing around. "There's smoke!" she cried, catching sight of it billowing from the church roof.

Her mother gasped. "It's the church! Oh my goodness, call the fire department!"

Grabbing her daughter's hand, she pulled her to the closest phone booth, one on the corner. She fumbled in her purse for a coin, found one and dropped it into the slot.

"…No, I don't know how long it's been burning."

The fireman on the other end grunted. "It's on the corner of what?"

"Twenty-first and Sycamore."

"Yeah, someone'll be right there." He hung up.

"Mom, what if someone's inside?"

"Don't say that. I'm sure there's no one there now. I don't see any cars in the parking lot." They stood on the edge of the sidewalk shivering and looked up at the black cloud of smoke rising ominously and blotting out the sunset.

A few other people began gathering, muttering to each other. An old Greek woman, numb with shock, stared first at the flames and smoke at the upper windows, then started wailing. "Better my house should burn than the church!"

A few parishioners coming for the vespers service pulled up in their cars, parked and got out, saw the flames and shouted and wept and didn't know what to do.

"Where's Fr. George?" someone said.

"Why is God doing this? – It's Christmas Eve!" A woman put her face in her hands, crying.

They were all powerless to stop it.

In the midst of his prayers, Fr. George heard the loud screeching of a fire engine siren coming closer. He expected to hear it fade away into the distance and cease disturbing him. But it didn't. It drew closer; then he heard the truck's noisy motor loitering in the street and its official radio talking. He crossed himself and kissed the Nativity icon, preparing to go out and see what was going on. Just one final look around his beloved church. It was so beautiful in the shadows, with only the oil lamps lighting up the gleaming gold on the iconostasis. Saints looked down from the walls, their faces full of the peace and joy which comes from loving Christ.

The firemen hooked up their hoses to the hydrant, ready to blast through the church's double doors. Fr. George walked peacefully out into the midst of them and stopped. A throng of troubled people met his eyes – firemen, strangers, parishioners… He stared, and they stared back.

"You were in there?" said one of the firemen in disbelief.

Fr. George nodded, speechless.

"Excuse us," said another fireman. "The building's burning, and we're going in." He raised his pick-axe to bash in the door.

"Please," said Fr. George, "don't do that." He caught the door handle and held it open for them.

They stormed inside like Viking warriors, ready to tear the church apart.

"I don't see anything burning," one of the men said slowly.

Another craned his head towards the ceiling. "The smoke was coming from the roof, but I don't see... " Only an icon of Christ Pantocrator gazed down at them from the dome, untouched.

"Maybe there's another floor up there."

Methodically, they walked around, testing the walls, sniffing for fire, feeling for heat.

"There're some stairs here," one of the men called out suddenly. He ran up them. At the top was a tiny room with three large bells hanging in it. There wasn't a hint of fire anywhere.

"All right. What kind of trick is this?" asked the fire chief, his hands on his hips as he faced Fr. George outside. "Who called us up? Nothing's burning in there."

"But look," said the girl who first had smelled the smoke, "look – those are flames!"

Every head was raised, every eye saw the brilliant strokes of fire against a darkening night sky. They clearly leapt from the church's roof. No other buildings were near enough to be on fire instead. As the people watched in amazement, the tongues of fire reached out into the sky, quivered there, thinned out and were gone.

Crossing himself, Fr. George thanked God. Now he knew exactly how to turn his people's hearts toward the true wonder of the Nativity. Through this symbol sent from Heaven, their blinded eyes might suddenly see and understand the marvel – the paradox – of Christ's Birth among men.

A larger crowd than usual gathered in the church on Christmas morning, all of them still confused and awe-struck by the mysterious fire of the previous night. There could be no doubt it was a sign from God, but what did it mean... ?

When Fr. George stood before them, prayer rope in hand, ready to preach his sermon, he took up the service book and opened it. "Let me read to you what it says in the Katavasia for the Nativity. Then I think you will all understand the holy symbol sent by Christ yesterday." He read, "'The furnace moist with dew was the image and figure of a wonder past nature, for it burned not the youths whom it had received, even as the Fire of the Godhead consumed not the Virgin's Womb, into which It had descended. Wherefore, in praise let us say, let all creation bless the Lord and supremely exalt Him unto all the ages.'"

Tanya Middle

DEDICATED TO ST. SERAPHIM'S PARISH IN RUSSIA.

Chickens pecked noisily in the yard, attracting the attention of a gray cat who crept slowly towards them; but seeing that they were too large to pounce on and too silly to be worried over, he sat up and washed his face.

From across the muddy path which might have been called a street, a dog started barking; and only then, as if the dog's voice were its cue, did the rooster crow to welcome the sun, rising like fire from the beautiful blue waters of the White Sea.

Tanya, who had been up for an hour already, wanted to go and watch the rooster shouting out his call, with his chest puffed out and his mouth wide open; but in the other room of the hut, Xenia called for her.

The old woman didn't feel well; her eyes, which had troubled her for years, now were almost completely blind. Her hands and legs were stiff, her ears didn't hear much; but lately, it had been a sharp pain in the back that had driven her to her bed.

"Auntie, you must eat something," said Tanya.

Xenia nodded. "Whatever you wish, my child."

"Bread," said Tanya, hurrying back into the kitchen to get some bread and bilberries, with some goat's milk from the scrawny goat who lived in a shed outside.

Tanya stayed with the old woman while she ate—so slowly.

"I'll be going soon, my child—today," said Xenia.

"No, don't say that, Auntie! You're going to feel better after you eat. How about some mushrooms? Would you like that?"

"No, my child. Thank you, but I don't need mushrooms." She wore a half-smile on her face. "I'm so happy that I will soon be free," she said. "But, when I'm gone, Tanya, say your prayers. And go and visit the museum; see the faces of the holy martyrs who suffered here on Solovetski Island."

"Yes, Auntie, I will."

Xenia drank her milk, then smiled again. "I want to tell you a secret," said the old woman. "Sit down, my child."

Tanya drew up a little stool and sat.

"I want you to know, Tanya, I'm a nun," said Xenia. "I've been a nun now for many, many years."

Tanya's eyes widened in surprise; she leaned forward, almost toppling off the stool. "Oh, Auntie, I never knew!" She knelt to kiss Xenia's hand.

"I've been in hiding all my life," said Xenia, "and at last, when I found myself alone, after the faithful who had been in the catacombs with me had passed into God's hands, I came here to this blessed island where my sister Masha lived because her husband was born in the Ribalde settlement. I outlived them, too, so I took their orphaned child Tanya into my hut."

"Thank you, Auntie. I'm so glad you took me in!"

"I'm glad, too, my child. And now, dear, I'm going to follow those who went before me," said Xenia. She began to murmur her last prayers.

There was a lump in Tanya's throat as she carried away the few uneaten berries and the wooden plate and cup. When she came back into the room and sat by her aunt, Xenia took both her hands and held them in her own, whispering, "God keep you, Tanya, my child." Then she folded her hands peacefully, preparing to approach the divine Throne, and closed her eyes as if to sleep.

Tanya knelt beside the bed and kissed Xenia's hands repeatedly, until at last she bent her head and let fear and sadness overcome her. Tears rolled down her cheeks, and she sobbed with grief.

When she stopped and wiped her eyes, the room was quiet. The only sound was of her own breathing. A peaceful radiance surrounded the old woman's face, and Tanya knew that now her aunt was free forever. She had left the empty world and entered the glorious, everlasting one, to find the Saviour she had served all her life.

— * —◄◊►— * —

After the burial, Tanya went home. The hut was lonely with no one but herself to live there. She cleaned it and milked the goat, fed the cat, and gathered eggs from the hens. Yet the rays of sunlight all the while shining into Xenia's room showed it to be painfully empty.

Having finished her work, Tanya put on her worn brown sweater and stepped outside into the sharp, windy air. She began walking, hardly knowing where she headed, until she reached Sikirny Hill. Here, standing at the foot of Ascension Skete, she saw Solovetski Island spread below her. The majestic beauty of the land and buildings tinged with purple light from the setting sun all at once overwhelmed her with loneliness. The beauty couldn't hide the desolation of Solovetski Island. So many had given their lives to God in this place; even now, Xenia also. And she had been a nun all this time!

Tanya knew little about the Church. She prayed the prayers she had been taught, but she didn't know if she had ever been baptized. Most of the time it mattered little to her, but sometimes she worried about it because she feared what death would bring her. Death—it lay so close. And just beyond the sky was the world where Xenia's soul now lived, but she was too far away to comfort the child she had left alone.

Chilled by the wind, Tanya sat down in the grass, pulling her knees up and wrapping her arms around them to keep warm. Far away, the waters sang and the wind moaned; it seemed as if no one were there but herself.

She shivered. It frightened her to think of going back to the hut and finding it hollow and silent. The godly peacefulness of Xenia had gone, leaving only stillness. But the cat would be wanting to eat; she, herself, might choke down a potato. No, maybe just a little bread.

Tanya got up and started down the hill. As she walked, the darkness grew deeper, until at last stars appeared and sparkled with brilliance.

The hut was clothed in shadows. Once inside, she lit a candle and did her last few chores: feeding the goat, shooing the chickens into their coop, and feeding the cat. Then, after eating some bread, she put on her shawl and climbed onto the stove to sleep because it was a cool night.

Holy
New-Martyr
Archbishop
Eugene
(Zernov)

Holy
New-Martyr
Archbishop
Peter (Zverev)

Holy
New-Martyr
Archbishop
Ilarion
(Troitsky)

Holy New-Martyr Priest Nicholas (Derzhavin)

The next day was Sunday, and Tanya let herself sleep late, since no one else was around. When she awoke, she had missed the rooster's crow by a good three or four hours. The cat was meowing pitifully for something to eat, the chickens scratched and pecked to be freed from their coop, and the nanny goat stood very patiently waiting to be milked.

When these jobs were out of the way and she had swept the hut once quickly, Tanya put on her brown sweater and went to the museum. A girl cleaning the museum told her that it was closed on Sundays, but she let her in anyway.

"See the faces of the holy martyrs who have suffered here on Solovetski Island," Xenia had said to her.

It was the first time she had really looked at those faces, and she saw that they were beautiful—not in a physical sense, but in some other way. Their eyes seemed to shine with the grace humility had given them; somehow she knew that even while they had labored and been tortured in the prison camps, they must have blessed the hands that wounded them and loved and forgiven the poor souls who had been so evil to them. And maybe a few guards had seen their love and been converted by it.

All at once, Tanya began wondering again if she had ever been baptized. Why had her parents never told her? They had died too soon, perhaps; and Xenia had arrived, but she hadn't known the answer to the question either. All at once, it seemed terribly important to know.

When she had looked at all the pictures in the museum, Tanya went back outside; and as she walked, she prayed to the martyrs, making up sentences of prayer as she went along, as if she were having a conversation with those holy ones whom she entreated.

Most weekdays Tanya gathered seaweed for a living, but it was tiresome labor and she had always wished for a vacation from it. Many times she had thought of asking the fishermen if she might go with them to fish off the coast of the island Anzer, but they were gruff and frightening men, so she hung back.

Yet, today, with no one at home who needed her except the animals, she couldn't help considering the idea again. Surely her neighbor Luda would tend to the animals in her absence; Tanya spoke with her first, and that was easily settled.

But the fishermen were harder to approach.

"You—a woman—want to fish?" The tallest one, Sergei, looked incredulous.

"Women belong at home," said one of the others.

"Yes," said Tanya, "but I would so like to see Anzer."

The fishermen exchanged glances. "You want a ride in the boat?"

She nodded.

"But she'll be in the way," said one.

"If you promise not to try to fish, or to tag along behind us once we land," said Sergei, "you can come."

"Oh, thank you!" Tanya bowed her head to them.

Perhaps the trip would take her mind off the painful loss of Xenia. Everything on Solovetski Island seemed empty without her; it was as if she, in her love and gentle kindness, had been a part of the soul of the island. Surely she had been the soul of the hut. Upon entering it, Tanya always realized that; the difference her absence made was one which would heal slowly.

Tanya packed a bag, instructed her neighbor Luda once more about feeding the cat, and went to bed.

Many hours before dawn the next morning, she awoke and crept through the house, trying to eat a quick breakfast without disturbing the cat. Poor thing; he didn't know he was to be entrusted to someone else's care for a few days.

The fishermen were already shoving their boat into the water as Tanya arrived. They grunted their recognition of her, and Sergei wordlessly helped her step into the wobbly craft.

It was a beautiful morning. As they set out on the water, streaks of orange made their way across the deep blue sky, and the tossing surface of the sea mirrored their light.

Turning their backs to her, the fishermen pulled out nets and began their work. As if to trap the fish by silence, no one spoke. There was no human noise to mar the lovely sounds of God's creation—the wind sweeping across the waves and slapping them up against the little boat, and birds overhead crying out to welcome the new day.

Fish already filled their buckets by the time the fishermen and Tanya reached Anzer. Deciding to remain in the boat, they stopped only briefly to let her onto the shore.

By now the sun was out and shining more brightly than a golden cupola. Soft white sand formed a gentle sweep of beach where she landed, and not far from the shore stood a small house; passing this, Tanya found herself on a solitary forest path, where rays of sunlight, mingled with the motion of shaking leaves, formed a lovely pattern on the ground. The wind blew so gently in the forest that it almost sang.

True, this wasn't the boring work of gathering seaweed, or the sad aloneness of the hut, but it was very desolate all the same. The quiet and mellow rays of the sun made her think of the faces of the martyrs in the museum on Solovetski Island. She had read that the worst prison camps had been here, on Anzer. Many, many holy priests and bishops had blessed the land with the sacrifice of their bodies, soaking it with their blood. Many had worked, many had suffered; and something was left behind where they had been. Tanya didn't know what it was, but she almost thought she heard chanting in the air.

After dusk fell on Anzer, the silence of the deserted island was complete. Seeking shelter, Tanya sat in the little house by the shore; and here she spent the night on the stove, after eating bread and mushrooms for supper.

She awoke later than she had meant to, at first unable to recall where she was; but, climbing down from the stove and catching a glimpse through the window of the waters outside, she instantly remembered.

Today Tanya had decided to visit the sketes on Anzer. As she wandered through the quiet, tumbledown buildings, she tried to imagine them full of busy monks hurrying to and fro, until at service-time they

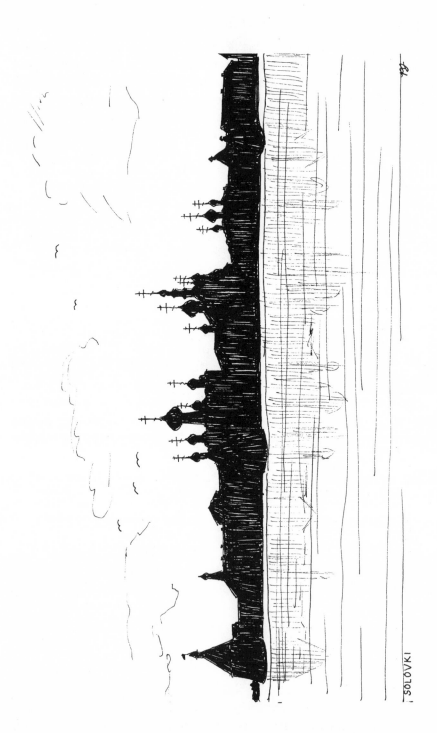

SOLOVKI

all grew peaceful and prayed with their whole hearts.

By the time she approached Golgotha Skete, the noonday sun already shone high overhead. Tanya stopped for a small snack before going on to the church. Seated on some grassy roots beneath a clump of white birch trees and eating some fresh berries she had picked, she all at once paused in the middle of chewing and listened. A bird's voice was almost lost in the wind; but that wasn't the sound she listened for. It was the sound of chanting—she was sure of it this time. The faraway words, mingled with the wind, made her feel like crying. A clear picture of Xenia came into her mind, for the voices were like those of a choir of nuns.

Tanya got up quickly, sure that the singing was more than simply her imagination. There, straight ahead, from the spaciousness of Golgotha Skete it drifted towards her.

Timidly she entered the skete, which was filled with rubble and bricks. A small group of people stood chanting. One of the girls held a cup of incense, with which she made the sign of the cross in front of several small icons that were lined up against a pile of bricks. Another woman held a video camera, something Tanya had never seen, and she didn't know what it was.

She watched them for quite a while, in awe and joy, without their noticing her presence. It seemed amazing to her that these holy people were here, carrying on the legacy of faith which the martyrs and monks had left behind.

"I thought no one else was on this island," said Tanya, when at last they finished their prayers and, turning, saw her.

"We just arrived today," said one of the girls.

"You chant so nicely," Tanya told them, "it reminded me of my aunt."

And when they asked kindly about her aunt, she told them more, not even holding back the fact that she had been a nun. They crossed themselves to hear it; it was joyful news that the catacomb church had existed in so many places. Then they talked more about the Church, and one of the girls, whose name was Lydia, offered Tanya a paper icon, which she took thankfully.

"I don't know if I was baptized as a child," she said. "I wish I knew, but no one can tell me."

Lydia and Yelena related how their group had joined a church under an archbishop in Greece.

"We have a tiny chapel in Moscow," said the third girl, Xenia.

"It sounds far away," said Tanya, "but I wish I could see it."

They immediately invited her to come with them when they returned to the city, and she smiled and agreed to think about it, as she walked with them through the skete collecting pieces of brick and rocks.

That night they all crowded into the little house to sleep. Yet sleep wouldn't come to Tanya; she was too full of wonder at the new faith she was just now learning existed. From their words and actions, she saw that these people truly loved and trusted in God, and with His love they also loved every stranger and neighbor they met. Their kindness to her was like Xenia's kindness had been—founded on the rock of their faith in Christ Jesus. Tanya felt eager to find out more about this faith; she wanted to erase the doubt about her baptism—to be baptized and to know that she was a servant of the Heavenly Father.

When dawn's lovely colors dashed like spilled paint across the sky, the young women awoke and ate a quick breakfast before traveling further in their boat. Tanya told Lydia and Yelena and Xenia that she wanted to join the church they had told her about, under the archbishop in Greece.

They began telling her more, answering all her questions, until she was convinced that her decision had been from God. Tanya might be sorry to leave beautiful Solovki, but the little chapel in Moscow beckoned. She would be a nun, too, who rather than fleeing the world, entered into the midst of it to endure from it suffering that would cleanse and purify her, as it is written: "For Thou hast proved us, O God, and by fire hast Thou tried us even as silver is tried by fire." (Psalm 65:10)

So Tanya gave her goat and chickens to Luda, taking only the cat with her when she left.

And to differentiate her from the other two Tanyas in the parish – Tanya Big and Tanya Little – everyone called her Tanya Middle.

The Path to Christ

"I see that in every way you are very religious. For as I walked around and looked carefully at your objects of worship, I even found an altar with this inscription: To An Unknown God. Now what you worship as something unknown I am going to proclaim to you." Acts 17:22-23

"For if you live according to the sinful nature, you will die; but if by the Spirit you put to death the misdeeds of the body, you will live, because those who are led by the Spirit of God are sons of God." Romans 8:13-14

THE ROMAN EMPIRE, 55 A.D.

Though the day had been hot, the cool of evening penetrated the room where Emilian Priscus sat. A lamp burned, dispelling the darkness but leaving shadows; the shadows suited his mood.

It ought to seem peaceful here in this room, empty as it was except for Emilian Priscus himself, filled only with the quiet of evening that still held the small noises of insects and birds and servants further away in the house. Peace . . . Yes, he had sought peace, but it was a precarious thing, lost as soon as a man laid hands on it.

Perhaps peace wasn't what the god had in mind for His servant, or perhaps He found something lacking in Emilian Priscus' worship of Him. It was difficult to guess how He wanted to be worshiped, and so it would be even harder to correct any mistakes Emilian Priscus had made in His sight, with no one to tell him what they were.

Half against his will, Emilian Priscus cast a glance at the shadowed niche in the wall at the far end of the room. No statue stood there now, and he couldn't even remember which god the niche had held when his father died, they had changed so often. One month his father was worshiping one god; the next month, or soon thereafter, he would cast that god's statue into the rubbish heap and embrace a new philosophy. He tired of gods quickly, although he had always been eager to try new beliefs.

Maybe it was his father's constant variance that had led Emilian Priscus to choose the god he tried to serve. At his father's death thirty years past, he remembered ordering his father's burial according to the rites of his current god, whichever one it had been, while he himself took part of his inheritance and set out for Athens.

But that had been a mistake. In choosing a distant city in which to distance himself from his father's memory, Emilian Priscus had accidentally chosen the one where his father would feel most at home.

Thinking of it, he could still shudder, though he was old enough to smile at himself for doing so. The Athenians amused themselves with philosophy as other men did with simpler things, food and drink and sport. If ever there was a place for a young man confused over religion to find a god he could worship, Athens wasn't it.

Except that, oddly enough, it had been. Because in Athens, walking in the temple district, Emilian Priscus had caught sight of an altar labeled simply: To An Unknown God.

And that had been his answer, put in his path by the god Himself.

"Am I wanted, sir?"

Blinking, Emilian Priscus returned to his lamplit room, summoning a nod for Menodorus, his secretary of so many years, standing in front of him with his writing tools in his hand and a patient expression on his face. "Yes, you are. I was just . . . considering the past."

In Menodorus' eye, Emilian Priscus saw a glint that was the closest his secretary ever came to a smile. "Of course, sir."

"Be seated, Menodorus. Whose letters remain to be answered? Lavinius', I suppose?"

"Yes." Finding a stool behind him, Menodorus dragged it closer and settled himself on it. "He's sent three since you last answered him, sir."

Emilian Priscus permitted himself a sigh. Half a year ago, his son had promised to return within two months. The two grew to three, the three to four. Now promises no longer came, although letters did, at regular intervals. Dutiful as Emilian Lavinius always was, his hastily-dictated lines had one main theme. "Which is better in the god's sight, do you think, Menodorus? To give alms to the poor, who value the smallest coin, or to send money to Lavinius, who casts it away without thought?" Not that there was really any question of not sending money to his son, Emilian Priscus thought.

Pursing his lips, Menodorus weighed the question. "Since the young man is your son, sir, he can hardly be cut off from your support. The sums you send him could be lessened, though."

"If I did that, most likely I would force him into debt, if he isn't in it already. Ah, but I realize my age when I think of the way the young live these days. Men were simpler when we were young."

Menodorus inclined his head. "So they were."

"But who am I to judge them? Who can say what pleases the god? I'll send Lavinius the usual amount."

When he had dictated his letter to Lavinius and Menodorus had left him, Emilian Priscus sat for a while longer before calling his slaves to prepare him for sleep. Who, indeed, could say what pleased the god? Everything Emilian Priscus did, he did hoping. A man who served an unknown god followed his conscience, for only the god knew how He liked to be worshiped. Emilian Priscus had to guess.

Morning brought a fresh wave of supplicants to Emilian Priscus' estate. With the distance they had to walk, through the dust and heat, they impressed Emilian Priscus, and few of them left without some token of his respect. Poor as they were, the god had made them, and if He had placed Emilian Priscus far above them and had given him wealth, and had spread abroad his reputation for kindness, hadn't He done it for a purpose? The least Emilian Priscus could do was fulfill the purpose, so far as he understood it.

Today, one face that he'd expected was missing, and Emilian Priscus reached out to stop a man as he turned away with a bit of Emilian Priscus' silver in his hand. "Where is the widow Ignacia? Is she well?"

"She is, sir, as far as I know."

Unusual for her not to come, then, unless she'd finally succumbed to her age and no longer felt able to hobble all the way to Emilian Priscus' estate. In which case a servant might ride into the city to see her...but the man was continuing.

"She's joined a new faith, sir, and they'll care for her."

"What faith is this?"

"Something the Jews thought up, I think. Shall I mention to her that you asked after her, sir?"

"Yes, do." Did the man realize how little sense he was talking? Ignacia, a Roman, joining a Jewish sect, when the Jews refused even to visit non-Jews?

Although now, with his office full of the poor, he was forced to put the matter aside, Emilian Priscus thought of it again when he retired to his private rooms later in the afternoon. The old Roman widow, wrinkled and bent, associating with Jews. Well, if they would take care of her, Emilian Priscus should be glad for her. Sighing, he laid aside his outer robe and sandals, and drew the stool where Menodorus had sat the night before up to the empty niche. When he prayed to the god, committing his troubles to Him, he brushed the edges of the peace he longed for.

If only he trusted the god more. How often he'd wished he knew more about Him; once, in frustration, he had descended so far as to ride into the city and halt at the steps of Jupiter's temple, but he hadn't gone in, because he knew too much about the Roman gods to respect them. Although his lapse of faith shamed him, he thought that his own god, about whom he knew nothing but in whom he tried to place his trust, had even forgiven him that lapse when he knelt before His empty niche and confessed it with tears, begging for mercy.

What other god offered mercy? The graven gods of the empire were capricious, merciful one moment and unforgiving the next, but the unknown god, who could neither be bribed nor placated with sacrifices, forgave when entreated with tears. Emilian Priscus knew this, as he knew that only a truly merciful god could endure a worshiper like him, who so often failed in his piety.

When he failed, tears were waiting, and the god's help and comfort.

If only the god knew how it felt to be human, Emilian Priscus would think in the moments when he felt farthest from Him. If only the god had been hungry and tired and understood how it was to be these things, and how a man's temper might be short at such times. If only He knew about suffering.

The most disquieting thing was, sometimes when he prayed, Emilian Priscus had the feeling the god *did* know. But if he would not cheapen the god by imagining Him no better than human, then how could He be anything but pure Divinity?

Leaving his thoughts, he rose and paced across the room to summon a servant, instructing him when he came: "Go into the city and call on a certain widow, Ignacia. Menodorus will give you directions to her house. Take a basket of food and these coins, give them to her, and see that all is well with her."

Jewish sect or not, the poor widow could barely walk, and she had been dependent on Emilian Priscus' charity almost since he began worshiping his unknown god. What if the man he'd asked about her today had been mistaken? Surely the god, who had not abandoned His less-than-perfect servant, would not want Emilian Priscus to abandon Ignacia.

Not until dusk, as Emilian Priscus sat in the courtyard listening to the soft sounds of an evening shower, did the servant return. "The woman you sent me to is well, sir, and thanks you for your kindness."

That was good. The servant's news set Emilian Priscus' mind at rest. "Your report is welcome. You've done well. Go now, I have no further need of you."

Dismissed, the servant hesitated until Emilian Priscus looked up. "What is it?"

"Sir, a man returned with me from the widow's house. Do you wish me to send him in?"

From the widow's house? One of her new friends? Reminding himself of his loyalty to his god, Emilian Priscus fought a surge of curiosity. Better to send the man away, perhaps, or offer him refreshment in the servants' quarters, but that might be a breach of hospitality, when he'd walked all this way in the wet, probably with the intention of seeing Emilian Priscus. Surely, with the god's help, Emilian Priscus could resist for an hour or so whatever new faith the man embraced. "Yes, I'll see him."

His response didn't seem to set the servant's mind at rest. Emilian Priscus watched him lower his eyes and move his lips, shaping things he might say, until he blurted out, "Sir, he's a Jew."

"Ah." Now things became clearer. "Won't he enter the house? Does he want me to go out to him?" Not pleasant, in the rain, but possible.

"No, sir. He'll come in—he already has, in fact—but I don't know... I thought you should know."

Emilian Priscus inclined his head. "Thank you. Offer him fresh clothing, if he wishes it, and send him to me in my private chambers."

Apparently the Jew didn't care for fresh clothing, for he came in still damp from the rain, with beads of it glistening in his hair. A slender man, younger than Emilian Priscus by a decade or so at a guess, with a Jewish nose and a smile that kindled in his dark eyes as he gestured to his damp clothes. "It isn't that I lack respect for you, but I didn't want to inconvenience your servants."

"I respect your decision, of course." Emilian Priscus watched the Jew take in the chamber with a quick glance, pausing on the god's empty niche for an instant, but not long enough to seem curious.

Finishing his brief survey, he turned his full attention on Emilian Priscus. "I'm glad you received me. My name is Xenos, I'm a Jew originally from Thessalonica, but now I live here. The widow Ignacia, for whom you were so kindly concerned, has mentioned you to me more than once."

Facing this Xenos, Emilian Priscus felt himself the object of an even more lively scrutiny than that given his room, and he found himself at a loss for words. What did a man say to a Jew who professed himself glad to break the laws of his religion that forbade him to visit a non-Jew?

Maybe too many of his thoughts showed in his expression, for Xenos spoke directly to his concerns. "If you're thinking that I shouldn't be associating with a Gentile, I beg you to set your mind at rest. God has shown me that no man is unclean or impure in His sight, for He created all of us."

"Yes, I believe that too." Emilian Priscus admitted it with caution.

Xenos' eyes strayed again to the empty niche. "I see that you have no idol set up. Which god do you worship?"

As little as he knew about the Jewish religion, Emilian Priscus thought they believed in one god only, and with that thought he wondered whether Xenos might understand his own beliefs better than some of his fellow Romans did. Still, explaining about the god to a stranger didn't come easily, and Emilian Priscus offered a prayer to Him for the right words.

"I believe in one god." He paused, watching a dark flicker in Xenos' eyes, and resumed again, saying what the god gave him to say. "Once, when I was young, I went to Athens, and there I saw an altar standing apart, with no graven image above it. At the time I didn't know which god I should put my trust in, but I hoped that in Athens I would discover the true one, and I believe that I did. The altar I saw was dedicated to an unknown god. I've never known His name, but I pray to Him, trying to follow what I hope is His will, and He helps and comforts me." Maybe he'd said too much; already he regretted the last part, expecting to see scorn on Xenos' face for a Roman's enthusiasms.

He saw nothing there but excitement, and the Jew took a quick step forward, reaching his hand out for Emilian Priscus' sleeve before he remembered himself and let it fall, though his eyes still shone. "Now I know that the Spirit inspired me to come here to you. I think this god that you worship without knowing His name is also the one that I worship."

The Jewish god! Emilian Priscus stared at him.

"You see, there's only one God, He Who created the heavens and the earth and everything in them. Of course, you believe that too. God Himself gives life and breath to all men, and He sets each man in the place where he may most easily seek for God and find Him, because He's never far away from us. You've found Him, although you don't know His name, but I think from what you've said that He has revealed some of His nature to you. He's a God of mercy and love, and He loves us so much that He sent His only Son to earth to become flesh for our sakes."

Here Emilian Priscus interrupted him. "How is that possible? The god is divinity." Even if Emilian Priscus had sometimes felt that the god knew what it was to be human . . .

"Anything is possible for God. He took flesh and remained God. In His human form, He suffered death, but it had no power to bind Him, and He arose, and through Him our sins are forgiven."

Mercy and forgiveness of sins, that sounded like the god, and yet . . . "But this is the Jewish god that you're talking about. I'm a Roman. How can our gods be the same?"

Xenos smiled. "I told you, God placed you where you would be able to find Him, even without knowing His name. God is the God of everyone, both Jews and Gentiles."

As the widow Ignacia must believe. As this Jew must believe, to be here. And why not? As Xenos said, anything was possible for the god— for God. Even forgiveness of sins and resurrection from the dead. This must be the god Emilian Priscus worshiped, the merciful god. He had revealed Himself in a stranger way the first time, in Athens when He permitted Emilian Priscus to see His altar. Why should He not reveal His name to Emilian Priscus through a Jew?

Reaching out, Emilian Priscus touched Xenos' sleeve, never wondering if he might defile him by it. "Stay here in my house for a while. I pray that you will stay here and tell me more of this God."

To which was he more dedicated, Bacchus or Venus? Of late, to Bacchus, Emilian Lavinius decided as he frowned into his cup. No, he hadn't been a good servant of Venus lately. To Bacchus he remained devoted because he brought forgetfulness.

Forgetfulness of self most of all.

Until his father's next letter came, he lived on borrowed money, lent him by this friend or that friend, with promises of returning it when he could, if he ever could. When the letter came that Lavinius had been expecting for close to a month now, then he could afford a debauch in grand style, serving Bacchus and Venus at the same time, and worry about his debts when his wine-stupor wore off.

Which might be never.

Cup in hand, he wandered out from his lodgings into the street, without a thought that he wore nothing but his tunic until a servant came pelting after him with a robe and sandals. That made him presentable, and he had a muddled idea that he'd arranged to meet a group of friends somewhere at about this time, but that might have been yesterday, or it might be tomorrow.

As he neared the marketplace, its bustle and shouts enfolded him, and he lounged against a nearby building, savoring his wine. If it was the best, he'd become accustomed to it in the time he'd been away from home, for it no longer tasted as splendid as it once had. And he restrained a sigh as two women of indeterminate social status, but probably lower than his, crossed the street to avoid passing him. Well, they might think a young Roman aristocrat worth avoiding, if they couldn't tell how deeply Lavinius had proven his devotion to Bacchus today.

Strange that he should want forgetfulness. Young as he was, not unhandsome, with friends who had introduced him to all the most expensive and exotic delights of this city sufficiently far from home . . . and had never mentioned that in half a year or so of grand living a man grew used to the taste of good wine and sweet lips, and longed for something else, something new.

Or at least for the old things back again, the simpler pleasures of home, cast aside in the rush for sophistication.

Moving into the marketplace, Lavinius bumped up against the stall of a rug-merchant, grazing his elbow in the process, and stood rubbing it and blinking at the merchant, who looked like little more than the pale blur of his face and a darker blur of hair. "Worldliness is death," Lavinius informed him.

"I know."

"What?"

"I said, I know."

Turning his cup in his hand, Lavinius considered that. "How do you know?"

A movement rippled across Lavinius' blurred vision; the merchant might have shrugged. "The things of this world are empty, and emptiness leads to death."

There, he'd chosen the right word. Empty. Savoring it, Lavinius shoved away from the stall and ambled on, weaving around the common folk in the market. Empty pleasures, empty service to his chosen god and goddess, Bacchus and the Lady Venus. For certain the rug-merchant had the right of it.

Another week, another borrowed purse. Waking in the early afternoon one day, Lavinius dragged himself up from his bed and crossed the room, finding a bowl of water there which he could dump over his head to clear it. Though it did nothing for his headache, he could think around that.

Emptiness and death. The night just past Lavinius remembered in snatches: the cool metal of a cup, the swirling garments of a dancer.

And the same in store for tonight. Seized with restlessness, he walked to the window and stood looking out at the people streaming to and from the market, wondering how many of them, like the rug-merchant who'd spoken to him, understood that worldly life and death were the same.

But the merchant had sounded as if he accepted it, and Lavinius couldn't. Was he to go on immersed in pleasures, never caring that some inner part of him that he'd hardly realized existed withered and died?

Leaving the window, he called for a slave to bathe and dress him.

This time, with so little memory of the rug-merchant's features, Lavinius found himself wandering the marketplace peering into stalls, at a loss until he recognized a voice behind him and turned to see the merchant showing a woman one of his rugs.

That cast of features, something about the clothes . . . so the merchant was a Jew, but Lavinius had made up his mind already and approached him anyway, no matter that many Jews counted themselves more learned and more intelligent than most Romans.

Whatever his thoughts, this Jew greeted Lavinius with a neutral expression, in that voice that Lavinius remembered. "What can I do for you, sir?"

"You can answer a question, if you would."

Now the merchant regarded Lavinius with greater interest. "I'll try, of course. What is it?"

"You told me that you know the world is death."

"Ah. Yes, I remember."

So calm he was about it, infuriatingly so. "What have you done about it? If you know that, how can you go on living as if it weren't so?"

With a touch of his fingers the merchant smoothed the corner of a rug, but his eyes never left Lavinius'. "I worship God, Who is able to resurrect men from the dead."

"I see." Then it was the merchant's Jewish religion that consoled him. Fighting a disappointment which he told himself he had no reason to feel, Lavinius turned away.

"Sir!" Leaning over his rugs, the merchant called after him, waiting for him to turn back. "I don't think you do see. I'm talking about the Messiah, the Christ, and He doesn't show favoritism. You see me as a Jew, and you're right, but that's not all I am. I belong to the Way."

"The Way." Living here in the city, Lavinius had heard the gossip. "That's just another Jewish sect, isn't it? You have a leader who died a criminal's death, and you claim—" Breaking off, he swallowed most of the rest of the words, because his thoughts had just caught up with his clumsy tongue. "You claim your leader rose from the dead. Is that possible?"

"I know men who saw it themselves."

"And you say he can raise others. Is it just physical?"

"No. He can raise men from spiritual death to life in Him."

"Then I—no." Slowly Lavinius focused again on the merchant. "Your leader was a Jew, wasn't he? What would he want with Romans?"

The merchant shrugged. "I don't know, but He wants them. He offers forgiveness of sins and eternal life to all who believe in Him, Jews or Greeks or Romans." With a thoughtful frown, he studied Lavinius. "If you're truly seeking resurrection for your soul, God can give it to you."

"You call him God. What about the gods and goddesses? What about Venus and Bacchus and—"

"Those are false gods."

Oddly, that reassured Lavinius. If a man served false gods, what did he expect but emptiness and death? Lavinius had found what there was to find. But if he served a true God, wouldn't he find fullness and life?

Drawing a deep breath, he faced the rug-merchant. "Will you tell me where I can learn about the true God?"

Emilian Lavinius wrote to say he would be home within three weeks, and although Emilian Priscus knew he ought to rejoice at the news, it filled him with apprehension. What would his son, cosmopolitan sophisticate that he must now be, think of the Christ?

He might think anything. If he greeted Emilian Priscus' attempt to explain with an indulgent, half-mocking smile, Emilian Priscus would not be overly surprised, and then he would know to keep his mouth shut, that Lavinius was not going to listen to him. But however Lavinius answered him, Emilian Priscus felt he had to make the attempt.

Most likely Lavinius wouldn't approve of Emilian Priscus' redoubled alms-giving, or of his frequent rides into the city to visit the church there and listen to Xenos, who had turned out, not surprisingly, to have the gift of teaching.

Lavinius wasn't asked to approve, only to accept, Emilian Priscus reminded himself. A man didn't answer to his son...but it would be more difficult to live a life in Christ under the critical eyes of a young pagan.

But with God anything was possible. Whatever happened with Lavinius, Emilian Priscus would pray to God to help him endure it. The God of mercy, Who answered the prayers even of a groper like Emilian Priscus, would hear him.

Laying aside Lavinius' letter, Emilian Priscus rose to order the first preparations for his son's return.

Not far in the distance, Emilian Lavinius could see the estate baking in the sun, and he slowed his horse, trying to prepare himself to greet his father. What would his father, pagan Roman that he was, think of the Christ?

When Lavinius explained his reasons for going home, they had all agreed that he should go. He'd told them, his fellow believers, that he'd left home to escape his father's authority, and that, having repented of the wild life he'd been leading, he thought he should return. So he was, but before he left to come home, his father's most recent letter had arrived, with a welcome sum of money, enough to cover Lavinius' debts, his journey, and as generous a contribution to the church as he could afford.

What was he going to say if his father asked how he'd managed to dispose of all that money in the week before he left? If he said he'd given it away as alms, which was mostly true, his father would approve, if he believed him, but he wasn't likely to believe him, and anyway good Christians didn't say things that were mostly true. They said things that were true.

There, Lavinius had made his decision. As politely as he could, he would tell his father the truth, and see how his father reacted to it. After all, why should Emilian Priscus complain? He believed in one god himself, his nameless god. If God granted Lavinius the right words, maybe he would even be able to persuade his father to believe in the risen Christ.

As long as his father didn't berate him for attaching himself to what he might call a Jewish sect, although it wasn't. If that happened, Lavinius prayed he would be able to restrain his temper.

Jews don't pray with Gentiles, he could say. But in Christ, we're all one, Jews and non-Jews. It isn't a Jewish sect. It's Christ's church.

While Lavinius thought, his horse had been closing the distance to the house, and before he felt prepared for his arrival Lavinius found himself dismounting in the courtyard, handing his horse's reins to a servant who said, "When you've refreshed yourself, sir, your father will be waiting for you in his private chambers."

Help me, Lord, Lavinius thought, and went inside.

Emilian Lavinius looked older, more sure of himself, Emilian Priscus thought as his son entered the room with a firm step and his head held high. Whatever had brought him home, it wasn't poor health. Crossing the room to greet him, Emilian Priscus embraced and kissed him. "I'm glad to receive you here, Lavinius."

"I'm glad to be received, sir." The answering pressure of Lavinius' arms against his father's ribs felt fervent enough, but his smile, to Emilian Priscus' eyes, looked forced.

"I see that you're well."

"Yes. And you, sir."

After that, there didn't seem to be anything more to say, but Emilian Priscus struggled to dredge up something suitable. "Did you find your time away from home profitable?"

Lavinius' eyes, startled and wary, flicked up to Emilian Priscus' face, and his tongue came out to moisten his lips before he answered. "More profitable than I expected, sir."

"Oh? How so?" Not in a monetary sense, if his requests for money had meant anything. In what sense, then? God help him, what might he have done?

Glancing down, Lavinius adjusted the hang of his sleeve, which also, his father noticed, served to hide his face. "I—um—no longer worship my old gods."

Emilian Priscus allowed himself a sigh of relief. "Yes, I have some-

thing similar to tell you."

"What?" After a quick glance at the empty niche in the wall, Lavinius looked up to meet his father's eyes. "Don't you worship your unknown god anymore?"

"I said I had something similar to say, not something the same. I worship the God I always have, but I've discovered His name."

"Oh." Frowning, Lavinius moistened his lips again. "May I speak freely, sir?"

"Please do." Before Emilian Priscus spoke to his son about the Lord Jesus, best for him to discover what Lavinius now believed and hear whatever he had to say, he decided. Then, with the Lord's help, he might know better how to explain the truth to him.

But his father's response didn't seem to reassure Lavinius, and he stood for a long time in silence, maybe arranging his words, with deepening frown lines carving themselves in his forehead.

At last he seemed to make up his mind. "You may have been able to guess, sir, that I wasn't living as you might have preferred me to live while I was away."

That much had been easy enough to guess.

After a pause in which Emilian Priscus forbore to comment, Lavinius continued in a cautious tone. "For most of the time I was gone, I was a devoted follower of Venus and Bacchus."

Despite his prayers, Emilian Priscus felt a coil of tension winding into his stomach, and his mouth filled with the cloying taste of apprehension.

"However, I came to see that that god and goddess were leading me to a living death, and I wanted to be resurrected from it."

To what else did the worship of false gods lead, Emilian Priscus thought, and approved of Lavinius for realizing it. In spite of his increasing fears, he said in as loving a tone as he could manage, "Then do you now worship Jupiter?"

Lavinius' mouth opened, and his eyes went dark with some emotion, but he struggled with it, and none of it showed on his face. "No. Why should I?"

He shouldn't, of course, and Emilian Priscus swallowed bile. *Let me learn the worst now,* he begged the Lord; he hadn't imagined how it would hurt to hear his son speak so coolly of gods and goddesses when he, Emilian Priscus, would be ready to give his life for the true God. "Do you follow the Stoic philosophy, or have you chosen to worship the emperor as god?"

Lavinius glared. "No!"

If there had been wine within reach, Emilian Priscus would have snatched for it to cleanse the foulness from his mouth. As there was not, he could only entreat the God of mercy to enlighten his son. "Who, then?"

Taut, furious, humiliated, and on the brink of tears, Lavinius choked out, "I said, I worship the Christ, the Son of God."

"What!"

"I said, I worship the Christ, the Son of God." The Christ, the Son of God; Lavinius had repeated it twice. Doubter, Emilian Priscus accused himself. How had he forgotten that with God anything is possible? "You can't mean the Lord Jesus, the Saviour of the world. Are you speaking of Him? The risen Lord?"

Lavinius was staring at him. "How did you know?"

"How could I not know? Lavinius, my son, I told you I had learned the name of my unknown God."

Other Titles from
ST. NECTARIOS PRESS

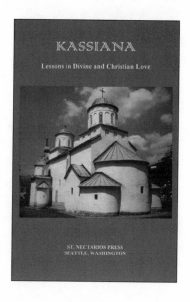

KASSIANA:
Lessons in Divine and Christian Love
From the Collected Works of
Bishop Nikolai Velimirovich
The Lessons in Divine and Christian Love
is in the form of a letter from Archimandrite
Callistratus, Abbot of Mileseva Monastery
in Bosnia-Herzogovina, to his spiritual
daughter, the nun Kassiana. Before her ton-
sure she had blasphemed God in desapir
over her unsightliness as a hunchback. These
Letters bring her back to God. The book also
contains the story of Julia, who became the
nun Kassiana.
80pp. Illustrated Paper $8.00

THE SAINTS OF ANGLO-SAXON
ENGLAND
(9th to 11th Centuries)
Lives of many lesser-known, early saints
of England from a period not well
known by Orthodox Christians – the last
flowering of sanctity before the Norman
Conquest of 1066.
3 volumes approx. 100 pages each.
Illustrated
Paper. $8.50 each.

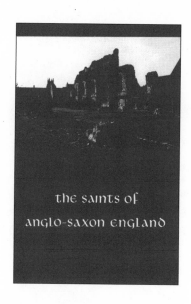

Katie Visits a Monastery
The description of a young girl's first visit to a monastery. An excellent introduction to Orthodox monasticism written for young people – suitable also for Sunday school use. Contains exercises and puzzles at the end.
49 pages. Illustrated
Paper. $6.00

A Pilgrim's Guide to
The Holy Land
FOR ORTHODOX CHRISTIANS
This inspired account, written by Orthodox Christians, follows as a pilgrim in the footsteps of our Saviour through today's treasured Holy Land. Biblical texts provide a guide for travel according to events in the life of Christ as one visits shrines, monasteries, mountains, and rivers. Photographs, maps and historical narratives present the Holy land as it is actually seen today.
192 pages. Illustrated
Paper. $22.00

A PILGRIM'S GUIDE TO
THE HOLY LAND

ST. NECTARIOS PRESS
and BOOK CENTER

Publishers and Distributors of Quality Orthodox Materials

A WIDE VARIETY OF BOOKS FOR ALL AGES
Wholesale and Retail

also BAPTISMAL CROSSES, GREETING CARDS, and more

Retail catalog of over 600 Orthodox books, cassette tapes, crosses and other items.

**WE ACCEPT VISA, MASTERCARD,
AMERICAN EXPRESS AND DISCOVER**

Call *toll-free* for catalog and orders: 1-800-643-4233 (U.S.)
Outside U. S.: (206) 522-4471 – FAX: (206) 523-0550
E-MAIL: orders@orthodoxpress.org
Web site: www.orthodoxpress.org
or write to:

**ST. NECTARIOS PRESS
10300 ASHWORTH AVENUE NORTH
SEATTLE, WASHINGTON 98133-9410**